The Unbearable Sheitness of Being

Thaddeus Lovecraft

&

Nick Faulder

Published by Pillar International Publishing Ltd.

www.IndiePillar.com

ISBN: 0957459858
ISBN-13: 978-0957459854

DEDICATION

To the Mancationers – long may the tradition continue.
– Thaddeus Lovecraft

I would like to dedicate this book to my wife Jacqueline, whose complete lack of tolerance and patience with my writing career has manifested itself so clearly over the past eleven and a half years that I personally have perfected the honourable qualities of long suffering and perseverance - qualities for which I am known today; I hope to deal with honesty and integrity in the near future.
– Nick Faulder

CHAPTER ½

Detective Chief Inspector Finagle Brush had spent two years tracking, baiting, catching and banging to rights The Ramsgate Racoon. He deserved a well-earned rest. Sitting in his office, nursing a cup of tea and perusing *The Hendon Gazette*, an advertisement winked at him: full board and a week's fishing on the Isle of Arran. Ideal, and a perfect way to put nasty memories on ice – memories of blood, shredded trousers and the murderer's hallmark of a mackerel jammed down the victim's throat. Without a second thought, he made the booking.

*

Following a hearty breakfast in a small, homely guesthouse, he set forth in an inflatable dinghy from the little harbour, carrying a parcel of sandwiches and a canvas bag marked *evidence* in bold black. Brisk air filled his city lungs, the sea swayed lazily in a near calm. Overhead, seagulls, terns and gannets jostled for space in a seaside opera. The prospect of dinner and a malt whisky later that evening completed his sense of well-being.

He reached into the canvas bag, pulling out an assortment of bomb-making odds and ends.

'Ramsgate Racoon,' he chuckled, as he inserted a

detonator and timer into a block of Semtex. Fellow officers had suggested *The Thanet Turbot* and *The Deal Eel*, but he pulled rank and named the killer *The Ramsgate Racoon*. Brush was his own man. He put on ear defenders and dropped the explosive device over the side.

It was at this moment the mobile phone next to his crotch began to vibrate.

'Damn it!'

He rummaged in his trousers and jammed the phone up to one ear, just as the water exploded, sending mackerel, crabs and a shopping trolley skywards through a flock of screaming gulls.

'Brush here,' he said, his exposed ear ringing from the explosion.

'... Brush... murder... Mint... con...'

'What?'

'... Commiss... parcel... choirboy...'

'They've conned a hard choirboy into murder with a mint parcel?'

'No... listen!'

Brush shook his head until the ringing stopped and tried again.

'Sorry, can you repeat that?'

'It's The Yard, Brush, Commissioner Madover speaking. There's been a murder at Castle Montgomery.'

'Not Lord Anton Montgomery?'

'Yes, and you know what this means?'

'Do I?'

'Pay attention, Brush! Lord Anton Montgomery fought our corner on the police complaints board. Without his help those charges of cannibalism at Paddington Green police station would have stuck. This is serious. Someone killed him and it might have been to get at us. DC Lapdance is at the scene but he's out of his depth. You're the closest man we have.'

'I'm on the case, Commissioner. Tell Lapdance not to do or move anything.'

'Very well, I'll call him now. It's in your hands. I need a result and I need it fast, so don't let me down.'

With the dinghy slowly deflating, and progress further hampered by copious amounts of stunned fish and seabirds on the water, Brush rowed towards the quay. This was indeed serious.

*

Taking the late ferry to Argyllshire, Brush cycled through the night and arrived at Castle Montgomery shortly after dawn. Parking the chequered blue and yellow Raleigh Shopper next to the lodge, he gave the Montgomery family home careful scrutiny - wind-racked trees, stables, outbuildings adjoining a curtain wall and towering over everything, surrounded by lawn, a lichen-encrusted, stone keep. The Isle of Arran could be clearly seen across a white-flecked sea, as could the Mull of Kintyre. It was all starkly beautiful, if a little sombre.

Placing cycle-clips in the front basket, he crunched up the gravel drive to the main door. A uniformed constable stood guard.

'Good morning, Constable. Brush of the Yard.'

'Mornin', sir. DC Lapdance is expecting you.'

He nodded, stepped over the threshold into a vaulted hallway and strode between flanking suits of armour. He stopped at a studded, oak door at the hall's end. Above the door, engraved in stone, was the Montgomery coat of arms – three otters couchant. Above that, a painting of a breaching killer whale with a leg hanging from its mouth. A diamante Prada stiletto confirmed gender. Brush remembered the extensive media coverage of the death of Lady Montgomery. Tragedy, it seemed, followed this family.

His musings were cut short when the door creaked open. A mass of unkempt grey hair above a stained, dark three-piece suit shambled through. The door was quickly pushed shut. The hair raised itself, revealing a lined face with bottle-glass spectacles wedged on a bulbous nose.

Brush had the impression the man wasn't actually looking at him when he said, 'Please don't put him in one of those black plastic bags, Hamish.'

'Who are you, and what are you on about?' said Brush.

'You know me well enough, Hamish Neaps.'

'I'm DCI Brush.'

'A DIY brush, you say? This is an inappropriate time for *another* door-to-door salesman. Be off with you!'

The shabby ensemble grabbed hold of a suit of armour and dragged it towards the front door. 'We have no time for your kind today,' he told the armour.

Brush watched with interest as both man and metal collapsed in a heap. He said, loudly, 'You've got the wrong end of the stick. I'm Detective Chief Inspector Finagle Brush of Scotland Yard, here to investigate the murder of Lord Montgomery.'

The man noisily extricated himself from a tangle of arms and legs. 'You have my apologies, Inspector. My eyesight isn't what it was; neither is my hearing – *and* I get a little confused at times.'

'Am I correct in assuming you are the butler?'

'Yes. Rob Roy MacGrip.'

'Right, MacGrip. Please take me to the officer in attendance.'

Brush followed the butler into the kitchen, then the cloakroom, but decided to retrace his steps, alone, back to the hallway when MacGrip led them into a bathroom, where he turned on the taps and proceeded to undress.

Brush eventually arrived at the entrance hall, hazarded a guess on the whereabouts of Lapdance and opened the door from which MacGrip had initially emerged. The great hall lay before him, complete with minstrel's gallery, family portraits and more warlike apparel filling the spaces between. DC Lapdance stood next to a huge fireplace. Close-by, a weeping teenager sat slumped in a chair. Even closer-by, a blood-stained sheet on the floor covered what was obviously the body of Lord Anton Montgomery.

'I'm Brush. What have we got, Lapdance?'

Good morning, sir. The son...' He licked a finger and flicked through a notebook. '...Nestat Montgomery, sitting here, was present when the murder took place. The local gamekeeper confirmed death by shooting.'

'The gamekeeper?'

'He's a criminal pathologist and owns a funeral parlour in Crimbletoon.'

'A Mr. Hamish Neaps?' Brush ventured.

'Yes, sir.'

'I've already been mistaken for him. But that's not important now. I see you've brought the young man here so I can question him.' He walked over to Lapdance and whispered, 'But I could have conducted the interview in another room. He appears to be very upset.'

'I was told not to do or move anything, sir,' said Lapdance, standing to attention.

'You mean he's been sitting here since yesterday?'

'Yes, sir.'

'I think a well-done is in order. Well done. Take a break. I'll call if I need you.'

The DC turned on his heel and left the room. Brush made a mental note of his dedication to duty, a commendation would follow. He stepped over to the sheet and lifted it.

He had seen many unpleasant things in his time but this ranked high in the top ten. What had been a head was now a congealed mass of blood, brains, hair, bone and a monocle. Something caught his eye, a business card protruding from the top pocket of the evening suit. He extracted it and read: Nightmares and Dreams – Thomas Edison Boyle.

'Mm, interesting.'

Replacing the sheet, he turned to Nestat. 'I'm sorry, and this must be a terrible shock, but in your own time, please tell me what happened.'

Nestat raised his head. Through sobs he said, 'I could

tell he was a bad one. I saw him on Scotland's most wanted.'

With a rustle of cycle-cape, Brush swept backwards in surprise. 'You recognised your father's killer?'

'Yes. My father, my fiancée and I were here when MacGrip introduced a door-to-door salesman. The man and his pet monkey came into the room and–'

'Hold on a moment – your fiancée?'

'Yes.'

'Where is she?'

'The man took her after he murdered Father.'

'A kidnapping! Lapdance never mentioned this.'

Nestat buried his face in his hands. 'I tried to tell him but he wouldn't listen. Every time I spoke he sang "will ye no come back" at the top of his voice. He said I mustn't do anything or speak until you arrived.'

Brush mentally scrubbed the commendation. 'Go on.'

Nestat wiped his eyes and continued. 'The second MacGrip closed the door the monkey ran straight to me and jabbed me in the neck with a needle. I fell over. I could see everything but couldn't move. It did the same to Sally.'

'Sally?'

'My fiancée. The thing was so fast, even if it only had one arm.'

'Your fiancée only has one arm?'

'No, the monkey had one arm.'

'Right. So you recognised the one-armed monkey from Scotland's most wanted.'

'No, not the monkey, although I heard the man call him *Spank*. He dragged his foot and dribbled.'

'The monkey dragged his foot and dribbled?'

'Not the monkey, the man.'

'I see. Please continue.'

'That terrible face, I'll never forget it – all flaky and blotchy. His hands were bandaged, more like claws than hands. That's when I recognised him.'

'The bandages gave him away?'

'No, not the bandages, his face – I recognised his face. There was a lot of wheezing, but I think he was laughing when he shot my father... when he shot him... five times in the head. He hobbled over to me and knelt down. His breath stank of raw fish. I've smelt it before in a sushi restaurant. He slapped me a few times on the face then dragged Sally away by her hair.'

'Sushi, you say. Was this man Thomas Edison Boyle?'

'His name is, if I remember it correctly, Doctor Wilberforce Slash.'

Brush caressed his chin, smiled and nodded thoughtfully.

Nestat's expression brightened. 'You've heard of him, then? Do you know where to find him?'

'I've absolutely no idea, but I've thought of a nickname.'

Nestat's eyes narrowed. 'If you don't find him, I will. And when I do, I'll kill him.'

Brush chuckled. The scrawny teenager didn't look as if he could kill a mouse. 'Of course you will, sonny, but in the meantime you'd better leave it in our capable hands – we'll find *The Montgomery Mink*.'

DEATH WEARS NO BRA
*SOME YEARS LATER, WEDNESDAY MORNING, VERY EARLY,
CENTRAL LONDON*

'Mink. Very becoming,' said Nestat Montgomery, making a small adjustment to his bowtie in a full length mirror. Save for the tiniest drop of blood encrusted in the winding mechanism of his Rolex Oyster Perpetual, nothing about Nestat suggested he had in the previous twenty-four hours killed seven men, a woman and a small dog.

His eyes strayed to the hotel king-size bed reflected in the mirror. On the wrinkled sheets lay a small book with faded gold lettering on battered and veined brown leather. Alongside the book, an empty shoulder holster. His gaze shifted back to Margot De Witte standing semi-naked at the bedroom door, the mink coat held open with one hand resting on her hip, the other arm extended towards him, holding a gun.

'Are you planning on cleaning my Walther, Margot, or do I take it that you're having second thoughts about our partnership?'

'This isn't about you and me. You know that.'

He turned, knelt, and began tying his shoelaces, never once making eye contact with her or the gun. 'Was it

8

something I said?'

She smiled. 'Since when did a Special Agent's salary stretch to Church's best?'

He raised an eyebrow. 'Special Agent?'

'Don't take me for a fool, Nestat. You don't work for Universal Imports. I did my homework. Did you?'

He stood. 'Let me see.' He buttoned his jacket. 'Thirty-five, former Miss America, cover girl for Follicle Magazine and pin-up of the month.'

Margot smiled. 'I'll give you ten out of ten for *that* homework. What about the rest?'

Nestat scratched behind his ear. 'Well, there was the little explosion in Islamabad and the small matter of the missing Africa diamond. Oh, and we mustn't forget the CEO who died peacefully in his sleep. Who carried out that post mortem, I wonder – *died peacefully in his sleep*? His legs and torso didn't share the same bed. Shall I go on?'

'I should have known. Top marks, again.' She sighed. 'But we do what we have to, don't we, Nestat?'

'And what's that?'

'What we're *contracted* to do.'

The spring-loaded knife hidden in his sleeve felt cold and useless. Not close enough. A few paces, a few slow inconspicuous paces and maybe he could cock the wrist, a left hand feint, and in an instant her jugular would redecorate the room. Knots in his back tightened. He had to get closer.

'Margot, why don't we take that book and sell it to the most foolhardy Russian we can find.'

'And then what?'

'We'd go deep undercover as Mr and Mrs Smith, fridge-magnet millionaires from Wisconsin.' A step closer, undetected he hoped.

'And in this grand plan, darling Nestat, when would you kill me?'

'Margot, please, you mistake me for another. Did the last three months mean nothing to you?' Another two inches of carpet covered. 'I would never–'

'Enough! One more step and it'll be your last. I'll not have that blade in your sleeve tickle my throat.'

'Ah, you noticed then.'

'Don't make this more difficult than it already is.'

Nestat pulled the knife from his sleeve and let it slip to the floor, far enough away to suggest it wasn't in play.

De Witte took a step back, the gun steady in her hand.

'I'm disarming, Margot,' said Nestat

'Yes – one of your sneakier qualities. Do something like that again and I *will* shoot you.'

Will, an element of doubt? He held on to this crumb of uncertainty. Time, he had to play for time – and think.

De Witte cut across his thoughts. 'Look, I don't actually want to kill you,' she said, using the gun now as a pointing device rather than a tool of execution. 'And I don't want to die either, by the way. You're one of the good guys, Nestat. I mean that, really I do. You're noble. You've got a wrong to right - Slash, Sally, your father and all. You have a right to shoot Slash and get your vengeance. Damn it, Nestat. Damn you!'

'Look, Margot, are you going to shoot me or not?'

Her expression remained determined, and yet the body language altered slightly: shoulders slumping a little, a slow intake and release of breath, a flicker of sadness in her eyes. In short, resignation.

'You have such a beautiful face,' she said, softly. 'How could I shoot you when you have such a beautiful face? Turn around.'

'Margot, please?'

'I won't say it again. I don't want to look at you when I do this.'

A single bead of sweat traced a line from his temple, stalling at a stubbled jowl.

'Face the wall otherwise you'll leave me no choice.'

Her words were cold, a different Margot from the passionate woman sharing the bed, a dressing table and a chair less than an hour earlier. The soft exploring lips were set and resolute, the heavy-lidded, sensuous eyes unflinching. And all because of a wretched book he never wanted to get in the first place.

Turning to face the wall, he considered the chances of making a grab for the knife. Maybe he'd take one, possibly two hits? In a coin-flip world there was a chance of survival. This last crumb of hope was snatched away when she kicked the blade into a corner of the room.

Taking a deep breath, he exhaled slowly. A heavy weight lifted from his heart, a weight he didn't know had been there, until now. Maybe this was the right time to die. No more painkillers; no more chasing Slash's ghost and the memory of Sally; no more grinding his teeth in hotel bedrooms; no more fear. His knees slowly buckled.

'Do it.'

'Nestat, before I–'

'Just do it, Margot – for pity's sake, do it now!'

He felt warm breath on his neck and caught a whispered word – *Bigginil.*

A world of pain exploded in the back of his skull and Special Agent Nestat Montgomery entered whiteness. No life flashed before his eyes, no long tunnel with Granny waiting at the end, no angels' chorus calling: absolute white and a sense of *being* whilst, at the same time, not existing at all – and a faint odour of herring.

'Hello? Hello?' His words echoed and faded.

So this was death? And yet no sign of God, no sign of Buddha with a ticket for re-incarnation and, thankfully, no ungulates with bifurcated tails. But there was something resembling a corporeal presence. He could feel his feet standing on solid ground. His arms and legs, still in a tuxedo, were stunningly black amongst the all-encompassing white. Was this it, alone here in a tuxedo for eternity? These thoughts drifted as he lit upon the notion that his father might be near. Maybe it was an ante-room for the next life? Did he have to call; would a door open in the whiteness?

'Dad, Dad! Are you there? It's me, Nestat.'

A blur punctured the white, like ink leaking into milk. A shape emerged, resolving itself into human form.

'Pull yourself together, boy,' said the person.

Although brusque and deep, it was a woman's voice. The image became clearer. A straw boater adorned with fruit; a long, dark pigtail resting on the shoulder of a tweed jacket; matching skirt; heavy surgical stockings; lace-up shoes – all of it somehow familiar. But from where?

'Are you listening to me?' she said.

A sharp prod in the solar plexus followed her words. He grabbed the weapon and used it to pull her closer. It was an umbrella.

'Let go, boy! You'll have me over.' She swung a carpet bag, thumping him on the shoulder.

Nestat let go. 'You're pretty accurate with that umbrella. Who the heck are you? I know you. Do I know you? Is this heaven or hell?'

She hit him with the bag again, on the head. 'Pay attention, Nestat, we haven't got long.'

Nestat blinked hard and looked around. The white background filled with people, hundreds of people doing what people do – walking, talking, sitting – only in absolute white: white walls, floor, ceiling and furniture.

'Look at me!'

Her words passed him by. In the distance, a child with a red balloon danced around a man in a toga.

Harshness left her voice as she said, 'Nestat, please, look at me.'

He faced her, and the memory came. It came with a smell and a sound – old oak and beeswax and the slow, clonking tick of a grandfather clock … his father's study. And there, on the desk, a photograph of Great Aunt Nellie.

'You died when I was a kid!'

'Did I – do I look dead?'

'Where's Dad? Is-is Mother here?'

As everything had gradually come into sharp detail, so now the process reversed. Great Aunt Nellie's features blurred.

'What's going on?'

'Listen,' said Nellie, 'you'll be off in a jiffy so pay careful attention.'

'Off?' Nestat's head began to swim. Nellie was melting back into the white.

'You're Special Agent Nestat Montgomery, so do what you've been trained...'

The words were indistinct. 'Do what?'

'... *Liber Nigellus,*'

Nestat caught this before empty, white silence enveloped him once more. The smell of herring lingered.

STOP THE WORLD
SUNDAY EVENING, QUEENSWAY, WEST LONDON

Tommy rubbed the stubble on his chin and tried to focus on the men sitting alongside him at the bar: two men with veined cheeks and red, bulbous noses. There were definitely two men. No, one man. Or was it two? They had asked a question, but he'd forgotten it already. In fact Tommy was struggling to remember anything, except that he had been drinking. Had it been seven pints, or nine? It didn't matter, more than four tankards of Badger Bolter threw mind and body into the realms of whirligigs and shipwrecks, and to make matters worse, a lukewarm Cornish pasty he'd eaten an hour earlier hadn't made friends with his digestive system. Internally and externally everything was on the move. An inner voice of caution said, "You need to leave the pub. You need to go home and sleep. You need to puke – and not necessarily in that order."

'What did you say yer name was again?' said the men.

Tommy swayed, concentrated hard and watched the two individuals fuse into a single person. 'Tommy, my name's Tommy.'

'I'm Ollie, by the way, since you ask.'

'I did?'

Ollie belched with his mouth closed, the cheeks swelling to contain the rush of gas. 'Thanks very much, Timmy, I will have another.'

'You will? Okay.' He called Cyril the landlord over and slapped a ten pound note on the counter. 'A pint for my friend, Oliver.'

The drinks arrived quickly, almost as if they were already poured and waiting under the counter.

Ollie took a couple of large swallows, half-emptying the glass. 'Y' know what, Timmy,' he said, wiping his maw with a sleeve. 'The minute I clapped eyes on ye I said to m' self, there's a decent geezer.'

'You did?'

'Yep. A right goodun.'

Tommy leant forward. 'Do I look handsome to you?'

Ollie's brow furrowed. 'It'll take a lot more than a few pints to get me—'

'Not in that way,' Tommy interrupted. 'I just want to know, friend to friend.'

'Timmy, you're more handsomer than Brad Pitt. I wouldn't think twice if I batted both ways.'

'Why did she leave me, then?'

'Why do they ever leave us, eh?'

Tommy burped and said, 'She left me for some rich prat with an even richer, titled daddy.' Briefly looking away, he faced Ollie again and said, 'We. Were. Engaged.' He had said each word as if it were a separate sentence.

'Was she a nice one, then?' said Ollie.

'Who?'

'The one who left you.'

'She was ... she was—'

Tommy felt the world move as his backside lost grip on the bar stool. Flailing out, he managed to gain purchase on the pie and pasty unit on the bar, and nearly dragging it off the counter, hauled himself back on the seat.

Cyril, the Landlord, moved quickly to wrestle the unit

from his hands. 'Steady on, Tommy lad. One more like that and you're out.'

Tommy waved a hand dismissively.

Cyril pointed to the door. 'I mean it. Last chance.'

Ollie put an arm around Tommy's shoulder. 'He'll be grand. Poor lad's been dumped by his lass.'

Tommy sucked the top inch off his pint. 'So you're name's Timmy.'

'No, my name's Ollie. You're Timmy.'

'Oh, I remember. Ollie, my good friend Ollie, I'll tell you why she left me.'

He shoved a hand into the pocket of his jeans and extracted a crumpled piece of paper. 'Penny's list: ten reasons why I left you, Thomas Edison Boyle. Number one – you can't hold down a job.'

Ollie nodded. 'Sure, who has a job these days? I'm on the dole meself.'

'I'll tell you, my friend.' Tommy swallowed hard. 'You mightn't know by the cut of me, but I was a financial high-flier.'

'Oh, I believe it. Thirsty work all this chattin'.' Ollie winked at his now empty glass.

'I was the dog's danglies at Chisholm and Chisholm.' Tommy leaned forward, almost giving Ollie a gentle head-butt. 'Never believe what you read in the papers. Insider trading – me? It was all a pack of lies. The Chisholms stitched me up and Chisholm junior took my woman.'

'Them Chisholms sound right bastards.'

'I want to kill them.'

'Too right, Timmy, and you'd be within y' rights – now, about that pint.'

'I can't kill them, though, because that'll be murder and another thing for Penny to put on the list. No, I'm going to kill me instead.'

'Of course you are, Timmy. I'll call the landlord over, shall I?'

'Number two: you drink too much.' Tommy picked up

the tankard and drained it. 'Yeah, right, drinks too much.'

Before a momentary increase in gravity saw him hit the floor, an inner voice whispered to Tommy – *If irony happens in a bar and there is nobody sober enough to witness it, is it still irony?*

His head cracked on the hard, flagstone floor. As he lay there, a murmuring of voices undulated in and out of his consciousness. Several Ollies requested that he honour his round, three Cyrils pointed accusingly and said, 'Last chance.' The world spun, dizzily, emetically, propelling Ollie and Cyril's faces in a loop before merging them into one scabby, shingles-ridden visage, that spun and laughed and spun and laughed … then exploded in a fit of bronchial coughing.

The floor stank of puke and bleach, but at least *it* didn't move.

WAITING FOR BECKETT
MONDAY MORNING, NOTTING HILL

Tommy woke to the sound of his brain thumping in time with his heart.

A beam of dusty light cut through a gap in the curtains. So, it was daytime. A fit of coughing sent him retching. He felt hollow and the side of his head hurt.

A few blinks and a bleary-eyed scan of the room: the grubby duvet, brown and beige, the cramped kitchen, blackened pots in the sink, a closed laptop upon a writer's desk-cum-coffee table, a single bulb hanging like a suicide victim from the ceiling.

'Home,' he heard himself sigh, with relief and disgust.

A creaky tap and the sound of running water behind the chipboard bathroom door gave him pause for thought. Home but not alone.

Lifting the duvet, he had a sniff and fiddled with his boxer shorts. Had he scored? No evidence there, just the smell of socks.

Maybe he had scored but had been too drunk to perform? If so, what was she like? Creaking to a sitting position, he scratched his chin with one hand and blindly reached for a packet of Paracetamol on the bedside locker with the other.

'Damn!'

The cold cup of coffee had been sitting there a week and a nasty greenish skin hung from the ends of his fingers; he wiped them on the duvet.

Swinging his legs off the bed, one foot crunched on a burger wrapper, the other on the remains of pita bread. He looked up at a grim print of Samuel Beckett hanging on the opposite wall.

'Keep a chair warm for me, Sammy.'

The sound of running water stopped.

What was she like, this mysterious morning toilet-dweller, a Russian shot-putter or French Model? French models couldn't exist in this rarefied air.

'Better have a drink, Tommy,' he heard himself say. 'Release the inner charmer, just in case.'

Tossing mottled cushions from the sofa-bed onto the floor, he located a bottle of vodka jammed between cushion and armrest.

'To drink or not to drink, that is the question? Whether 'tis nobler in the mind to suffer the slings and arrows of outrageous fortune or…'

One tilt of the bottle showed it to be empty, not even a drip. 'Oh, that's just friggin' great.'

Somewhere another bottle lurked. 'Where are you hiding my precious?' he said, fumbling under the sofa-bed. His wandering hands settled on something damp and underpanty. Recoiling, Tommy's addled brain suggested an alternative theory on the toilet enigma – perhaps it was Penny, spending a penny. Was it her in the bathroom? He edged towards the door and listened. No noise. In the silence he vaguely remembered being in the pub and being very drunk, but little else. Had he called her from the depths of despair, like in the past? Had she relented this time and come to see him?

He gulped, gripped the tarnished silver doorknob and twisted carefully, quietly. The door creaked as it opened.

His jaw dropped.

'Timmy, can't a man have a shit in private?'

He shut the door and opened it again. A man with greasy, grey hair, a heavily-veined face and a red bulbous nose was reading The Sun newspaper and having a crap in his toilet.

'Will yer look at that then,' said the man, folding the newspaper and showing Tommy a picture. 'She's a big lass, wouldn't y' say?'

She was very well endowed, Tommy noticed. He also noticed his toothbrush on the floor, a few spits of blood in the sink and that the man had hardly any teeth. With a shudder, he shut the door and leant back against it, trying to think. Remember. Remember. Who the heck is it?

A shout came above the sound of the toilet flushing. 'You're outta Cornflakes and vodka. I had a right hunger and a thirst on me this morning.'

The opening door pushed Tommy towards the sofa-bed. Jumping in, he gripped the duvet with both hands and dragged it up to his chin.

The man appeared, still tucking himself in and pulling up his fly. 'How about going to the early house for a few pints then?'

Tommy couldn't find words. He smiled and squinted, trying to remember the night before. The man didn't look menacing. That was something, at least. He was all bones in his dirty suit.

'Look, I'm really, really sorry but I must have been smashed. How do I know you?'

'Know me? We were best friends last night. Had a right good session we did. And didn't I bring you home when you banged your head?'

'Yes – right – of course. Look, I'm sorry but... I mean to say...'

'You're a queer one, Timmy.' The man picked up a teddy bear, Tommy's one-eyed teddy bear. He stared at a bit between its legs where stitching had come undone and poked a finger in the hole.

'Queer?' Tommy tightened his grip on the duvet.

'Yeah, queer. Like that geezer Rowan Atkinson.' He tossed the bear to the floor. 'So you're a writer, huh? You drink like one anyway.'

'I told you I was a writer?'

'Yeah, y' did, and that you was a big man in the city at one time. I'm Ollie remember? We met last night.'

Memories began filtering into Tommy's head. He was lying on the pavement and crying. Ollie had cradled and hushed him like a baby. A mixture of guilt, embarrassment and anger welled up inside. He'd told him how his parents had drowned after being forced off the road into a river by a drunken priest; about the Chisholms doing a bit of insider trading and setting him up to take the fall; how Chisholm junior offered a consoling shoulder for Penny to cry on – in bed. He'd told Ollie everything. Had he mentioned the list? His eyes swept the apartment, running over the detritus of weeks of neglect. Throwing off the quilt, he jumped out of bed, pulled his jeans from the floor and rummaged in the pockets.

'You looking for this?' said Ollie, pulling a crumpled page out of his pocket. 'I thought it wiser to hold onto it. This thing is poison. I read the bit on the back. Forget about it, lad.'

Tommy snatched the paper from his hand. 'I shouldn't have... you shouldn't have read it.' He unfurled the crumpled sheet, containing Penny's ten reasons to leave. On the reverse were the last six things to do before saying goodnight to the world. He'd ticked the first five. The final one, get "well and truly hammered for the last time" hadn't been ticked. He could do that now. At the bottom of the list he'd written *kill myself.*

'So are you gonna to do it?' said Ollie.

Tommy stared at the paper. 'Yes. It's time to switch my lights off.'

'That's what you kept saying last night. Switch yer lights

off. Isn't there somebody you can call? Why let them Chisel geezers get away with it?'

'Chisholms,' he corrected.

'Whatever. Don't give in like a wimp, Timmy. Call your woman Penny and talk. Fight back, man.'

Tommy threw the list on the bed. 'But she's not my woman anymore, is she? And I'm not a wimp. And who the hell are you to give me advice?'

Ollie's bloodshot eyes didn't flinch. 'You're not going to do it.'

'What do you mean I'm not going to do it?'

'I can tell. I've seen many a man do his self in. I did time in a real hell-hole and I've seen their eyes, the fear and the peace before they top themselves. I don't see it in you, and I've never seen one make a list before.'

'You don't know me. You have no idea what I've gone through!'

'Alright, Timmy, steady on.'

'Tommy. For Pete's sake, my name's Tommy!'

Ollie nodded and said, 'Look, I'm no fool. I'm just a drunk you met last night and that'll be that. Pay me that twenty quid and I'll be on my way.'

The teddy bear came into Tommy's mind, provoking an involuntary clench of his buttocks. 'Why do I owe you twenty pounds?'

'For the cab home. Cyril gave me your address and lent me the money. Cough up and I'll drop it in on the way.'

'Cyril gave you twenty pounds? I don't believe you.'

Ollie cocked his head. 'On the condition you never set foot in his pub again. It took a bit of cleaning up I reckon. He wasn't very happy last night.'

'Oh, right, that sounds more like Cyril.' Tommy opened a drawer in the bedside locker and extracted a twenty pound note from a jumble of money and empty painkiller packets. Whacking it into Ollie's open palm, he said, 'Thanks for helping me, Ollie, but I have things to get on with. You're welcome to the booze and cornflakes.

Goodbye.'

'Do y' want me to call back later and make sure you're alright?'

'No! No thanks.'

'Listen, Tommy Boyle, don't even think about it.' Ollie drew a finger across his throat. 'That bit I mean. You're not one of them losers. Work it out. Fight back. Be a man.'

'Thank you for getting my name right at last. Goodbye, Ollie.'

Ollie turned to go, leaving the scent of wet dog in his wake as the door shut. Tommy followed him and threw the deadbolt. Leaning back against the door, he punctuated the silence with a long exhalation. It was all very well making a list of things to be done before doing the deed, but now all the boxes had been ticked, and if Ollie was right, he should be feeling fear and peace. Fear, yes, but peace?

The various options he had considered as methods of despatch came to mind in shocking mental imagery: jumping from a high building, stepping in front of a tube train, diving off a motorway bridge. What would Penny think? What if she were called to the morgue to identify him after taking the tube train option, and they asked her, 'which bit of Mr. Boyle would you like to see first?' She'd want to forget that as quickly as possible – forget him. Hanging? He shuddered.

Maybe he *was* taking the easy way out, running away and being a wimp, just like Ollie had said? His big exit would engender nothing more than a wave of good riddance from Penny whatever way he did it. He, Tommy, would be forgotten, Penny and Chisholm would get married, have babies and him and his crooked dad would win game, set and match. Chisholm would win. Chisholm would win!

Fear gave way to anger. 'He's right, I am a ruddy wimp! I've given up. What happened to Tommy Boyle, raptor of the trading floor?'

He unlocked the front door and threw it back, knocking the phone off a side table in the process. He had to tell Ollie, to thank him. But he'd gone.

'I'm going to fight, Ollie,' he shouted towards the stairs.

'I'm going to fight,' he repeated quietly as he closed the door.

Picking the phone off the floor, he placed it back on the table. 'Grab the moment by the horns, Tommy.' He tentatively lifted the receiver and punched in the number. It rang a few times.

'Hello?' Penny's soft voice answered.

Tommy felt his stomach tighten as a finger hovered over the abort call button.

'Hello? Who is that?'

'I... I want to...'

He heard a man's voice in the background, getting louder.

'Hello?' said, Chisholm, 'Who's there?'

'Give the phone back to Penny, Gonzo,' Tommy blurted, his medulla oblongata taking on the conversation.

'Oh, so it's you, Boyle. Now listen here—'

'Don't get involved, Hector,' said Penny in the background.

'Yeah, don't get involved, Gonzo.'

'Tommy, don't call Hector Gonzo.'

'Great, you're back. Sorry, Penny. I need to talk.'

'Are you mad? I told you not to ring me. Have you been drinking already? Got all sauced-up and thought you'd try it on?'

'No, it's not like that. I've banged my head and got a bit of a hangover but I've not been drinking – not since last night. I... I'm... You still there?'

After a short silence she said, 'Yes, I'm still here.'

He swallowed hard. 'As of this moment I'm going to change, Penny I'm going to win you back.'

'Oh please. Don't do this to me, Tommy. I can't bear it

when you–'

'Really, Penny I'm going to get myself back together. I was about to do myself in when–'

'What!'

'It's okay, I'm not going to now. I've something to live for. If you hadn't left me I would never have known what it was. It's all become crystal... Please don't cry, Penny'

Tommy heard the phone hit a hard surface and the crying fade.

After a short silence Chisholm picked up. 'Listen up, you waster. If I ever catch you bothering–'

'No! You listen, Gonzo. I'm going to get Penny back. You're not getting away with it that easily, you slimy git. You still there – do you hear me, Gonzo?'

'Take my advice, Boyle,' said Chisholm in a sweet voice, 'change your mind about not doing yourself in, there's a good chap.'

The line went dead.

Tommy replaced the phone in its cradle and smiled. That was all the encouragement he needed.

AM I HERRING CORRECTLY?
WEDNESDAY MORNING, CENTRAL LONDON

Great Aunt Nellie had gone but the smell of herring hadn't.

'Don't fight, you're nearly dead,' said a herring-stained voice, attached to a bearded face. Male lips embraced his, sending a fishy plume of air deep into his lungs.

Strong palms pressed down on his chest. He heard counting. His thoughts raced. Where am I now? He convulsed, gulped in air and felt his heart leave the panicky fluttering of seconds before and resume a steady beat. The face backed away. Nestat climbed unsteadily to his feet and stumbled forwards, each step wobblier than the last, each blink granting him more information about his surroundings.

Blink. Same hotel room. Blink. A large, man rising from his haunches. He instinctively reached for the Walther inside his jacket, realising simultaneously that it wouldn't be there and that it wasn't. Blink. No Margot, no book. A quick and blurry assessment of risk told him the probability was high that the bearded man before him was trouble.

Clenching his fists, he lashed out wildly, missing the

stranger by a considerable margin. Losing his balance after a second hay-maker, he fell into his arms; they held him without any perceived desire to strangle or crush, allowing him to slip comfortably back into unconsciousness.

*

Nestat's eyes slowly opened. Above him, a blurred spider scurried between flakes of ceiling paint, making for a web-entangled bluebottle. A monochrome film of the last 24 hours played out in his mind: people with bullet-holes in their foreheads, making love on the bed, a dead dog, making love on the dressing table, an ancient book, making love on a chair, Margot holding his Walther and the surreal dream of Great Aunt Nellie in a big white room.

'Did Margot shoot me?' A dull, pounding pain made him grimace. Easing himself up onto one elbow, his hand explored the back of his head, no wound and no blood. Why didn't she kill me? A toilet flushed, sucking him fully into the present.

It only took a moment to make sense of his surroundings: one double bed, one lamp, one chair, one desk, TV on the wall, kettle, tea cups and saucers, adding to this the smell of potpourri cut with eau de body odour equalled a cheap hotel, not the one he and De Witte had checked into.

Rolling off the bed, he clasped the bedside lamp and waited, eyes fixed on the tatty bathroom door. Taps creaked into action, and interspersed with running water came a deep humming, sounding something like *The Ride of the Valkyries*. In the interminable time it took whoever it was to clean his hands, Nestat noticed on the lone table a half-empty jar of Rollmops and his olfactory memory caused him to be just the slightest bit sick in the mouth. Whoever was behind that door would most likely have a shaggy blond beard, herring breath and a lot of explaining to do.

As the washing and humming dragged on, Nestat

sought to expedite the situation. 'Come out. I have a gun!'

The taps creaked off. After a brief silence, a man's voice said, 'Err – no you don't.'

'Okay, I don't have a gun. But I have a lamp and know how to use it.'

The door opened a fraction and a large hand emerged, waving a white flannel.

Nestat tightened his grip on the lamp, and using the Oesterhagan technique he had learned in Murder by Furniture 101, readied himself to deliver the blow.

'Who are you?'

The flannel retracted and a shiny bronze badge and ID replaced it. 'I'm Hal – Hal Goth.'

Nestat checked them out. 'You're Agency?'

'Yep, Para-tech.'

'I've never heard of it.'

The man coughed and said, 'The guys on seventh.'

'Seventh? We only have six floors.'

'Sorry, of course you'd think that on your pay grade.'

'I beg your pardon?'

'Look, can I come out now? The ventilation isn't great in here and there's a bit of a log jam.'

'Okay, but edge out slowly with your hands up.'

The man, at least six-foot seven, emerged, his knuckles rapping the door lintel then scraping on the low ceiling. He wore a red t-shirt which may or may not have had the words 'I'm Horny' written across it – the first and last letters were obscured by a denim waistcoat. The sneakers were the white, casually unlaced variety, much loved by rappers, thugs and street charity collectors. The brown corduroys were faded around the thighs. His face was striking: surrounded by luxurious blond hair and a fine healthy beard, it was a strong face – a Hollywood leading-man kind of visage. But the blue crystalline eyes reflected a deep sadness.

'So, The Agency sent you to rescue me?'

'Something like that, yeah.'

'Well, I suppose I should thank you. So, thank you.'

Hal lowered one arm and tentatively extended it. 'Can I shake the hand of Nestat Montgomery? I'm a huge fan of your work.'

'Ah, what?'

'I've been following your stuff. You're all anyone talks about in Para-tech.'

Nestat almost offered his hand in return but retracted at the last moment, leaving Hal to descend into a frown. 'I've upset you?'

'I don't make friends that easily.' Nestat relaxed a little. 'So, where am I?'

'A couple of streets away from *The Grand*. I thought it best to get you out of there in case someone else found you. I lugged you into this place and told the guy on reception you were drunk.'

'That was good thinking. You can put your hands down now.' Nestat tossed the lamp onto the bed. 'You'll forgive me if I don't hang around.' Fixing his cufflinks, he pulled the dinner jacket from the back of the only chair and slipped it on. 'I have some business to attend to.'

'Yes, of course. You have to go after the book.'

Retrieving a comb from the jacket pocket, Nestat addressed the shameful state of his coiffeur in a cracked mirror. 'I'm not interested in that book. Slash. It's Slash I want.'

'It – the book – it wasn't in the room,' said Hal.

'Then Margot De Witte's got it and she's welcome. You didn't see any sign of her, did you?'

'No. Aren't you going to go after the book?'

Nestat rubbed the back of his head. 'She could have killed me but didn't. Why didn't she kill me?'

'I... you need to get the book back.'

'What for, I was only doing it as a favour for Jameson? "Get the book, Montgomery; give it to Margot De Witte, Montgomery." I wish I hadn't bothered, cost me nine bullets. As of now I'm back on the Slash file.'

'Jameson's dead.'

Nestat froze. Jameson was a good sort; he'd been his fag at Eton and had always gone easy on the leap frog.

'What happened?'

'Heart attack.'

Nestat shook his head. 'Rubbish, he had the heart of an elephant.'

'So I've heard, but someone cut it out and attacked it.'

Raising an eyebrow, he continued to fix his hair. 'So who's in charge now?'

'Clench.'

'Frisbee Frobisher Clench?'

'The same.'

'Mm, a curious choice. Wasn't he the tea boy?'

'Exactly. Don't you see, Nestat? It's all because of the book. You have to go after the book.'

The dream of meeting Great Aunt Nellie leaked into Nestat's thoughts: *Liber Nigellus*, the name of the book. But a blow to the head could do strange things he reasoned, like joining two incongruities together to become the body of an octopus with the head of Boris Johnson, the stuff of nightmares.

'What's so special about this book that so many people want it?'

'It's... You know the way time is curved but not curved? And... and... reality is concave.' Hal was making oval shapes and waves with his hands as his ideas sought to catch up with his words, leaving his communication skills and Nestat way behind.

'You must go after that book. It's too important to let fall into the wrong hands.'

'So you say, but I have one goal in my life and that is to—'

His train of thought was interrupted as his consciousness noticed something which his sub-consciousness had been banging on about for ages. He traced a line along his arm to the tip of a finger.

'Where's my watch?' Nestat had pressed Hal against the wall.

'Your watch? I dunno where your watch is. Ouch, flippin' heck that hurts.'

'Where is it?' He began to slowly break Hal's arm.

'*Gnurf.* I don't know where it is. Take mine. Please?'

Nestat loosened the hold, not enough to stop the pain, enough to keep the conversation keen. 'Come on, don't play games with me, where is it?'

Hal grunted and shrugged off Nestat's hand as easily as if it were a child's. The big man's expression changed: the eyes narrowed and the lips set hard with a slight downward curl. It was a cruel face. Nestat stepped back in shock.

'A woman has your trinket,' he said in an accented, guttural voice.

Nestat backed away as far as the small room would allow. He would have gone further but the wall was insistent.

'What the...?'

Hal collapsed to the floor, breathing heavily. Nestat grabbed the lamp from the bed.

'S-sorry,' groaned Hal in a weak voice, 'I'm not well. I change. I see things.'

Nestat considered throwing the lamp at him and making a run for it. 'Not well? You're possessed.'

'Margot De Witte has your watch. I saw it.' He panted heavily, raised himself up off the floor then fell back in a heap.

To Nestat, at that very moment, the only thing that made sense in that room was what Hal had just said. As the big man on the floor shook with a childlike febrile fit, Nestat regained his legendary sang-froid by way of a pill marked sang-froid. Dragging a blanket off the bed, he threw it over Hal. It was obvious – of course she had the watch; that's why she didn't shoot..

TANKS FOR THE MEMORY
WEDNESDAY MORNING, SOMEWHERE NICE

'That is excellent news, Wilberforce. You have done well. Contact me when the cargo is safely on the ship. Auf wiedersehen'

Baron Hardinger Von Sheit placed the Bakelite phone in its cradle and clapped his hands together as might an excited child or seal.

'Everything is going to plan, mein liebchen,' he squeaked, doing a lone waltz across a walnut floor towards an oversized mahogany desk.

The office, hewn out of solid rock, with a giant green aquarium taking up an entire wall, was filled with a veritable Louvre of artwork, amongst which the trained eye would recognise a gilt-framed oil on canvas of two swans, painted by Lucien Freud at gunpoint; a water colour of Nancy and Ronald Reagan smiling and waving; a pencil sketch of Hitler and Eva Braun and their dog playing Frisbee outside a bunker in Berlin. Upsetting the aesthetic, there also hung a portrait of a woman, not a Picasso, just disproportionate features amateurishly smudged over canvas. The Baron had painted this after destroying all photographs of his wife in a fit of madness, following her untimely demise.

A broad smile cracked his podgy face as he fell into a deep leather chair. He spun around a few times then perused a bank of switches on the desk. Below each switch were embossed letters in ancient Icelandic, and below these, yellow Post-it notes with, *Kleiner Donner und Blitzen – Grosser Donner und Blitzen – Blitzkrieg – Grosser Blitzkrieg mitt extras* and *Gute Nacht Vienna* written on them. His finger momentarily hovered over *Blitzkreig*. But the elation left him.

'Ach,' he said, turning the chair to face the huge glass tank filled with greenish liquid.

Easing his bulky frame from the black leather, he walked to the tank and pressed his nose against the glass. 'It will not be long.'

Tubes and cables gently swayed in the effervescing liquid.

Pushing the monocle to one side, he rubbed away a tear. 'The book is on its way here, mein liebchen. It will all be over soon.' He allowed himself a smile.

The donkey-bray of his door buzzer destroyed the moment.

'What!' A glance at a seventeenth-century Tompion and Knibb tall clock showed six-thirty in the morning.

The buzzing continued.

Struggling to tie the knot on his nightgown, he resorted to pulling it around his belly and holding it in place. Blowing a kiss towards the tank, he said, 'I promise I will shoot whoever it is at the door and dedicate it to you, my sweetbread.'

Thumping on the door followed the buzzing. Vexed to distraction, The Baron stubbed a toe on an ottoman as he left the room to the hallway. Swearing in three languages, he bit a fist to quell the pain. Witherspoon and Smythe had custom made the piece of furniture from the remains of a man called Otto.

'My lovely footstool,' he said, regaining his composure

and bending down to stroke the striped, velvet fabric. 'You must forgive my harsh words. It's what your mother would have wanted.'

Turning his attention to the door, now shaking under the blows, his brow furrowed as he strode down the hallway. 'Cease that infernal noise. I'm coming already!'

The thumping stopped.

Pausing a moment by a mirror to smooth a tuft of hair that had escaped meticulous grooming, he licked a forefinger and ran it over each eyebrow, then, satisfied all was in order, pulled a gun from inside his nightgown and opened the front door.

A young man stood on the threshold, bleeding from the neck. Closer inspection revealed he was bleeding from the knee also, and there might have been a slight trickle emanating from a hole in his right shoulder. This one might not need killing. This one might die by itself.

The Baron lowered the Luger. 'What do you want, and why have you disturbed me at this time in the morning?' He could see the wounded man was one of *his* men by the blue tunic and trouser ensemble, but he had so many men these days it was hard to tell them apart.

The man coughed up blood. 'Jones, Baron…I-I-I'm, Jones.'

'Put your hand over your mouth. This koala hair carpet is worth more than ten years of your wages.' The Baron thought a moment and remembered the name. 'You are supposed to be in London, aren't you?'

'The company jet flew me–'

'What! You mean you've been dripping all over my nice new jet?'

'S-sorry, sir, but Nestat–'

'Nestat?'

'Nestat Montgomery, a Special Agent. He hit us. Fred, William, Wendy – all of us.'

'So you have failed me.'

Jones lowered his head 'Yes, sir.'

'I already knew, so never mind. Plan C is going ahead.'

'We were plan B?'

'Yes.'

'Eh, who was plan A?'

'There wasn't a plan A. You haven't mentioned the dog; is the little chap alright?'

'I'm afraid Himmler is dead, sir.' Jones coughed up more blood, into his hands this time.

'That's a shame. Take off your jacket.'

Jones swayed. 'I'm cold, very cold.'

'Blood is leaking through your fingers. Take off your jacket.'

Jones grimaced as he removed the jacket.

'Now put it up to your mouth – just to be safe, mm?' The Baron smiled.

Jones complied.

'Now pop into the room over there. The floor is tiled. Get yourself comfy inside and then die. The cleaner can sort out everything later.'

'Y-yes sir.'

Jones dragged his body across the hallway, to a door marked *toilet*.

'That's the one. Good fellow.'

'C-c-couldn't you wake up the medic, sir?'

'It's very early and really, I don't think he'd appreciate it. At best you'd only have a fifty-fifty chance of survival. In you go.'

Jones opened the toilet door.

'Wait!' called The Baron.

Jones looked back, a glimmer of hope on his pale face. 'Yes, sir?'

'Are you married? Do you have a loved one?'

'I did. Wendy was my wife. Montgomery shot her.'

'Ah, that is a pity. In you go then.' The Baron raised the Luger. 'Or, I could finish you off now, if you like?'

'I'll take my chances in here, sir.'

'See you later. Oops. I mean goodbye.'

The Baron waited until Jones was safely inside before closing the front door. He said quietly, 'Nobody should have to experience what I've been through these past ten years. I have done you a kindness, Jones.'

With a sad expression, he walked back to his office, closed the door and went over to the tank.

'That was Jones, mein liebchen, he was a good man. You remember his wife, the one with six fingers and twelve superfluous nipples?'

The Baron's wife didn't respond – death and five thousand gallons of formaldehyde having curbed her conversational skills.

'We will be reunited very soon,' he whispered, caressing the glass with his fingertips

By pure coincidence, a pale hand floated into view, attached to an arm, but the body to which it was connected remained hidden within the bubbling, opaque liquid. Slender fingers brushed the glass. Only two inches separated the touch – just two, small inches. The Baron's mouth twitched, the monocle wobbled then fell and he burst into tears.

'I didn't mean to shoot you. It was an accident – a careless moment.'

The hand drifted away.

'Don't go. Please don't go!'

In response to his cry of anguish, a trapdoor opened above the tank. A bamboo pole descended and three monkeys in blue suits, sporting bell-boy hats shinned down. Amid chattering and squeaking, they began adjusting valves and switches on a console hanging by wires from the ceiling.

The Baron wiped his eyes and replaced the monocle. 'My little helpers, what would I do without you?'

One monkey, with a white feather in its hat, stopped what it was doing and peered down from the top of the tank; it cocked its head quizzically.

The Baron gave a single nod. 'If you would be so kind,

Obersturmführer Tricksie.'

The monkey gibbered, opened a lid on the tank and inserted a pole. After a bit of stirring, the hand came back into view, followed by the arm and then the whole body nestled gently against the glass of the aquarium. Her skin was slightly discoloured and the eyes bulged a little more than they should – but he could look at her.

'Slash will not let me down,' he whispered.

DON'T FORGET THE SHOPPING LIST
WEDNESDAY MORNING, CENTRAL LONDON

'As I said, I get visions,' said Hal, sipping his tea.

'You saw Margot with my watch?'

'Yes. I see things. It hurts.'

Nestat bobbed a teabag up and down in the cup until the inevitable moment where the string separated from the little piece of card. 'Of course she has the watch.'

'It started when I was a ch–'

'You see, she must have known what the watch could do. And what it means to me. It was my father's watch. That's why she didn't shoot me. Don't you see? She wants me to follow her. It's a sign, a message. Yes. A message.'

He fished for the teabag with his fingers. 'Ow!' A quantum thought leapt into his head. 'Of course – that's it! Slash is afoot. She's leading me to Slash.'

'Don't you want to know about my visions?'

'Another time, Hal Goth. I'd see a priest, if I were you. Thanks for helping me. I mean that.'

Nestat made for the door, then stopped, realising that the world was a rather big place and Margot, relatively speaking, was microscopic.

'Er, one more thing. In this vision, did you see where

she was?'

'I saw Spitfires and could smell cooking.'

Bigginil. She had said *Bigginil.* No she hadn't. Nestat's epiphany was complete. Only one place could boast a collection of WWII airplanes and some of the finest pie manufacturers in Christendom.

'Biggin Hill! She's gone to Biggin Hill.'

'Wait,' said Hal. 'You can't go.'

'Don't try and stop me,' said Nestat opening the door.

'I had to move you out of that hotel for a good reason.'

Agent Montgomery hesitated on the threshold.

'You're on the Shopping List.'

If ever there was a time for a jarring chord this was it. Nestat fairly wobbled as he faced Hal.

The Shopping List: such an innocuous name for something so deadly. Gibson and O'Malley started in the Agency with Nestat. They were on the list for two days before their decapitated heads rolled out of a dustbin in a backwater Iowa town. Nestat had mentored Houston, O'Dea and Williams. They lasted four weeks – a bad business involving a car crusher. Agents Charles Bacon, Wendy Milk and Francois Condom were never seen again after an actual shopping list was posted by mistake. The Shopping List was how the Agency cleaned house. Being on the Shopping List meant a contract on your life and one million dollars to the assassin who did the job.

'W-why am I on the list?' The sang-froid pills were running low and it looked like he wasn't going to be able to go back to the Agency and stock up.

Hal shrugged. 'Dunno. I got the news when you were unconscious. Order came straight from Clench. The whole place is rotten.'

'Damn nice of you not to kill me and claim the reward.' Nestat paced the room. If he still smoked he would have nailed a pack of Gitanes. 'Slash is behind this, I just know it.'

'Take me with you, Nestat. You can use me, use my

visions.'

'I work alone.'

'You worked with De Witte.'

'That was different.'

'I can help you.'

Hal reached inside his denim jacket and produced a coiled up leather holster and gun.

Nestat froze, but relaxed when the big man handed them over.

'They're yours – found them in the room.'

Nestat slipped off his jacket and fitted the holster. Caressing the weapon for a moment, he shouldered it and considered the situation. Hal could have killed him and been a million dollars better off, and yet he had helped and most probably saved his life. He might, at a pinch, prove to be a useful shield. And the visions could be handy.

'Do you know when you are going to change – get a vision?'

'Not really, but they tend to come when I'm scared or hurt.'

'Okay, Hal. You can come.'

Hal's face lit up. 'Thanks, I–'

'Just trust me, big guy, don't get between me and Slash. It wouldn't be good for you.'

He nodded, reached behind the chair and picked up a rucksack. Giving it a shake, he said, 'Got some useful stuff here.'

'How useful?' said Nestat, donning his jacket.

Hal grinned. 'An agency transponder tracker for starters.'

Nestat allowed himself a rare smile. 'You're full of surprises Mr Goth. Let's go.'

*

Nestat paid the cab driver and took a moment to scan Biggin Hill airport, now a different place from what he remembered as a lad. A few old buildings were scattered on the periphery, but glass and steel reflected the improved status of this Second World War aerodrome. Grandfather Wing Commander Octavos Montgomery had helped fight off Hitler's Luftwaffe from Biggin Hill, and it had been an accompanying trip with Gramps down memory lane that had brought Nestat here as a seven-year-old boy. Seeing Lufthansa cargo jets would have sent Gramps into a spin as the old boy wasn't the forgiving kind, as a fire and explosion at the Audi showroom in Crimbletoon bore out.

He turned to Hal. 'You're certain the fix came from this part of the airport?'

Hal checked the tracker's GPS display. 'Yep, from those buildings over there.' He pointed to a line of refurbished older buildings converted into small industrial units.

'And it's definitely from my watch?'

'For sure. She only switched it on for a second, but the emergency signal overrides all other input and registers permanently.' He frowned. 'The Agency may have picked up on it, though.'

'Better get a move on then.'

The building contained six units: Cornish Pasty Exports – Shepherd's Pie International – Scot's Pie Distribution UK – Import Export Transit Pies – Pies R Us and Hair Technician Equipment Wholesale. A large central sign above all of them read: Wend and Stodey Consortium.

'Which one is it, Hal?'

Hal fiddled with the tracking device. 'The signal came from behind the buildings.' He looked up. 'There's a sign pointing to toilets round the back. I reckon that could be it.'

They set off around the building, past extractor fans belching out wonderful aromas. Hunger gripped Nestat's innards; his last meal had been with Margot the previous evening and the food of love, Beluga and Dom Pérignon, hardly filled the stomach. But the thought that The Agency may have got here first put bodily needs on hold. He drew his gun as they approached the building.

Hal did another check. 'The signal came from the ladies toilet.'

Nestat nodded, walked to the door and pressed his back against the wall. After taking a second to mentally prepare, he moved quickly, kicked the door open and threw himself to the floor, all the while traversing the interior with his gun, prepared for unexpected surprises.

The toilet contained three cubicles, the type with a large gap under the door. No feet and no tell-tale signs of an assassin in waiting.

'Okay, Hal,' he said, rising to his feet, 'you check the cubicles.'

'What am I looking for?'

'Look for anything out of the ordinary, something alien.'

'It's a ladies toilet,' said Hal glancing at various dispensing machines, 'it's all alien.'

'Just get on with it.'

Nestat checked the obvious for a hidden message: the mirrors, two wash basins, waste bins and the ceiling. Nothing.

'What about this?' said Hal. 'Aussie women do it upside-down.'

'Are you looking at graffiti?'

'Yep. Try this one: Beware Lesbian Limbo Dancers.'

'Hal, be serious.'

'This is weird: Remember Milton Keynes.'

Nestat walked quickly to the door and threw it open, hitting Hal full force on the face.

'That's it!' Nestat studied the lipstick on the wall: Armani Rose, Margot's preferred.

'Milton Keynes?' said Hal rubbing his nose. 'Who'd want to remember that?'

'Never mind. We need to get to Margot's flat.'

The main door of the toilets slammed shut. Nestat leapt out of the cubicle, gun in hand, to hear a key turning in the lock. A hissing sound followed. Purple gas began to pour out of air vents.

'Hal, quickly, we've got to get out!

Hal responded by lurching out of the cubicle sideways and collapsing.

Nestat staggered towards him, eyes stinging and lungs burning. The gun slipped through his fingers, and with a final cough he joined Hal on the floor.

LESS CANCER, MORE TASTE
WEDNESDAY LUNCTIME, SOMEWHERE OVER ENGLAND

Margot De Witte traced a tapered, glossy-red fingernail over the gold lettering of the book. The plane shuddered in a pocket of turbulence.

'*Liber Nigellus.* Why does he want *you* so badly?'

Her eyes were drawn to the book. Easing a finger beneath the stiff, cracked leather, she turned it over. The first image startled her – a gothic demon holding a decapitated monkey by one leg. She snapped the book closed.

Something inside her said, "Don't read on. Give it to Slash."

She opened it again, making sure to take a few pages in with the cover.

It was a strain to read the tiny curlicue script; the Latin wasn't a problem as she'd mastered that amongst several other dead languages at Oxford, but age and wear had taken their toll on the clarity of the print.

"In the beginning was nothing. This was succeeded by generations of different nothings, each with their own unique abyssal depth and infinitely tiny emptiness. Then, there was a nothing which surpassed all other nothings by the simple expedient of being something. It was

not much — a nothing that smelled faintly of mint — but it was something and that, in the realm of everything, mattered. It was succeeded by a nothing that tasted of burnt garlic and, in turn, that was succeeded by a nothing that could have been described as 'sounding like a bell'."

She turned over a few pages. These words were in English.

'I roam the emptiness alone, a friend to the void. Every pain of your world is my ichor, every death without hope, ambrosia. I can't remember a beginning and will not contemplate an end. Such is my place — and yours, too, should you choose it. Reach out, submit to me and I will show you the sweetness of isolation, the ecstasy of abandonment, the pleasure of oblivion. I am the portal to every nightmare you ever had.'

The plane bumped and rocked. She shivered involuntarily as the icy tendrils emanating from the words in the book reached in and chilled her bones.

A shadow fell across the pages, startling her. Glancing up, she saw one of the blue suit brigade, the type that had escorted her onto the aircraft. He stood next to the seat, his brown leather flying cap differentiating him from the other blue suits.

'Yes, what do you want?' she inquired, with a contrived sweet smile.

He remained silent.

She snapped the book shut. 'Well, are you going to stand there like a clown or say something?'

Another woman alone on a plane with a strange man standing over her might be afraid. Another woman, realising that said strange man was staring down into her cleavage might at first be angry and then doubly afraid. De Witte was not another woman. She grabbed his groin and twisted.

'Mmmmph,' he whined.

She rotated her hand and let go. 'You'll have to speak up. I can't make out a word you're saying.'

His voice wavered between falsetto and tenor. 'Would

you care for a drink, Mrs De Witte?'

'Yes, double Jameson, straight.'

He nodded, withdrawing gingerly to the front of the plane.

Her eyes followed him before casting a disdainful glance around the cabin.

Margot de Witte wasn't good with planes. She owned several but couldn't name them. Ask her who won the World Series in 1904 and she'd tell you straight that nobody won the World Series in '04. Ask her who won the World Series in '94 and she'd tell you pointedly that nobody won the World Series in '94. At this juncture she'd recognise you're a smart-arse and politely smile and walk away. You'd realise that you're a smart-arse and, as she sashayed out of the bar, begin to question whether your aunt was right about you ending your days alone, soiling yourself in a one-room apartment. Baseball she knew, planes she didn't.

However, she knew enough to recognise a downmarket wreck when she saw one. This plane had propellers, maybe twenty seats and seemed to be leaking air through the doors and windows; it was cold, smelly and rattled – the hallmark of one man: Dr Wilberforce Slash.

She'd expected to see him outside the hotel, but instead had been bundled into a limo by three blue suits. One drove and the other two sandwiched her in the back. At Biggin Hill she'd expected him to arrive whilst waiting for the plane. No dice. Not having any idea where she was going, she'd asked some of the blue suits, but the reply had always been the same – 'Somewhere nice.'

She'd overheard them, though. They'd let slip one important detail. She'd left her message for Nestat. Something they wouldn't spot and which only he would understand.

The plane, as expected, was heading north. The fourth hand on Nestat's watch pointed north.

She gently touched the face of the Rolex. The blow had

been carefully delivered. He had to be alive. Something in her gut said he was alive, he was a survivor. She needed him, in more ways than one.

'This is the last time, Nestat,' she said quietly, pulling out the winder on the watch. With great care she turned it anti-clockwise then clockwise and waited ten seconds until a soft bleep confirmed the procedure. She had just put it back in her handbag when the cockpit door opened and the blue suit walked swiftly down the narrow aisle. He passed her the drink at arm's length then retreated hastily.

Her thoughts drifted to when Slash had passed her the Nestat file. The instructions had been clear as crystal: get to know the man, get the book from him and then ice him. No problem. When she'd retired to the comfort of a hotel, when she'd studied the file, there was something different about this man, something different yet familiar. He would never have known it, but they were at Oxford together. Not together in a physical sense, but together with a library-length of distance: her at one end, snatching glances at the scrawny boy buried in his book, the eleven-stone weakling who, in some counter-intuitive way, piqued her curiosity.

Then there was the agent, the man. How had Nestat changed so much in the intervening years? He had bulked up and seemed somehow taller. The shy innocence had been replaced by a cold confidence. Cold, but something warm beat within. He didn't show much emotion, but his eyes betrayed hidden fires beneath the surface. The eyes don't lie. Not since the unexpected demise of the former Mr De Witte in a freak accident on a bouncy castle had she felt so strongly about a man. Two weeks into working with him, she woke to the sudden and scary realisation that this was *the* man, the one. Co-incidentally, that was the day she learnt about Sally, his kidnapped fiancée. That was the day she learnt of his quest to shoot Slash five times in the face. That was the day she'd quietly resolved to help him do it.

In her mind, the scene would play out quite tidily.

Nestat would follow her to wherever they were going and together they'd save her father and wipe out Slash. Afterwards, there would be sunsets, horse riding and copious amounts of champagne then some more riding.

The plane lurched and pulled into a steep dive, passing from tranquil blue through thick, grey cloud. The seat-belt sign flickered on and off. On the horizon, a long landmass came into view.

'This is your captain speaking. We'll be landing shortly. Please fasten your seatbelts and extinguish all cigarettes and other incendiary devices.'

Would Nestat pick up on the watch transponder and the message? Would he pursue it and connect the dots to her flat? Did their time together mean as much to him as it had to her? She tilted her glass and swallowed the amber liquid in one gulp.

'He's an agent. He'll get it.'

As the plane rapidly lost altitude Margot noted the *Scottishness* of the landscape below: wild Atlantic water buffeting steep cliffs, shingle beaches, and white dots of sheep on the heather-clad hillsides, and rain pelting down onto a crumbling castle-ruin. Minutes later, the plane banked steeply and a runway, a large satellite dish and a zeppelin connected to a mooring mast came in to view.

*

'This is somewhere nice?' she said to the blue suit holding the large, black umbrella as they descended the stairs from the plane.

'This,' he said, not looking at her, 'is somewhere wet.' He gestured to the zeppelin with his free hand. '*This* will take us to somewhere nice.'

'Interesting,' she said, 'is Slash getting sponsored now?'

Painted on the side of the dirigible, a familiar actor, smoking a cigarette, and the legend – 'Middleton Lights: Less Cancer, More Taste.'

The blue suit shrugged. 'It's a recession.'

.

WHAT A DIFFERENCE A DAY MAKES

Tommy made another list, only this one didn't have 'kill myself' at the end, this one had Hector Chisholm with a drawing of the grim reaper next to it and Penny Green with two hearts pierced by cupid's arrow.

A few Paracetamol and numerous pints of water later and he had crossed off quite a few items already: clean bed-sit thoroughly and wash up – that took four dustbin liners and three litres of bleach; iron shirts, polish shoes and check suit for stains; shave, shower and trim hair with Man Care Grooming Set.

Finally, he was able to tog up ready for an apologetic visit to Cyril at *The Who'd a Thot It* pub before calling into the job centre. A quick once over in the newly polished full length mirror made him smile. A different man stood before him. His head still hurt a bit and the stomach felt very delicate, but overall, a thumbs-up.

Whistling *Big Yellow Taxi*, he locked the front door, checked his watch, one-thirty, and made off to the stairs at a jaunty pace. Sunshine struggled through the grubby windows of the stairwell, highlighting the dusty interior of the Victorian house. Normally a bit depressing, today

Tommy thought it rather beautiful.

Two flights of stairs later, a voice stilled his merry whistling.

'You got-a bit of steak-a for me?'

Tommy turned to see his fat landlord, Mr Viscotti, in a silk dressing gown and standing outside the door of his flat.

'Hello Mr Viscotti, I didn't know you were there.'

Viscotti flashed some gold teeth. 'I move a quiet and a silent – like a leper.'

'Like a leper?'

'Yeah, one of them little green little Irish boys that-a nick your money.'

Tommy racked his brain; he'd played this guessing game with his landlord before: green, Irish, money, 'You mean a leprechaun, Mr Viscotti.'

'Yeah, one of them.'

'I don't owe you any rent, do I?' Tommy had been out of it for some time and wasn't certain.

'Next week, Tommy. You look-a nice, nicer than I see you for a long time; you not going to work?'

'I don't work at the meat-packing factory any more. I'm off to get a new job. I've turned over a new leaf.' He beamed.

Viscotti's face fell. 'No more steak then.'

'Sorry, no.' Tommy's nose picked up the aroma of oriental cooking wafting through the half-closed door of the flat. 'By the smell of Mrs Viscotti's cooking, I doubt you'll miss my humble offerings.'

'Yeah, right,' said Viscotti, looking shifty. 'Mamma cook good but – well, I like the change now and then.'

'I'd love to meet Mrs Viscotti some time,' said Tommy, taking a step forwards. Viscotti blocked his way. Like the other tenants, Tommy observed the unwritten understanding that nobody was to mention anything about Viscotti's mail-order Filipino bride.

'She work-a the nights. She only get up to make-a my

lunch.'

'A good Italian woman, you're very lucky.'

'Yeah, sure,' he muttered.

'Tell you what,' said Tommy, 'I'll stop by the butcher later and get you a nice bit of fillet steak – my treat.'

Viscotti abandoned the blockade, walked over and grabbed Tommy's cheeks in a tight pinch, as if he was attempting to remove sideburns by force.

'You're a good boy, Tommy.' Releasing his grip, he held him at arm's length; his eyes narrowed. 'You still get trouble from them Chisel men?'

Tommy's teeth ground a little. 'Chisholm, Mr Viscotti.'

'Okay, but you remember when I said I can arrange they get a visit from my brothers, the ones who don't play nice?'

A high-pitched voice called out from the flat, 'Runch is on the table.'

'Gotta go,' said Viscotti hastily, the smile vanishing in a micro-second. 'You just a let-a me know, okay.' The door slammed shut.

*

Tommy headed out of Bayswater tube station towards Westbourne Grove. The hazy summer sun shone on busy restaurants, the scent of fresh bread, garlic and cumin wafting along the pavements. The memory of pasty and beer had put his hunger on hold, until now. A glance at the Punjab Punter as he walked past sent his stomach into a series of growling rumbles. Craning back to get a final look, he mulled over the idea of paying them a visit later when his train of thought collided with something deliciously perfumed.

'Oi, watch where you're going, dickhead,' said a well-dressed, attractive young woman getting up from the pavement.

'I'm sorry, I wasn't looking... Vicky!'

She brushed down her skirt and blouse. 'Tommy?'

'Sorry about that.'

'I'll live. I hardly recognised you. You look good, you clumsy git.'

'Thanks. Meet the new Tommy Boyle. I've seen the light.'

'What?'

'The Mormons.'

'You're jesting.'

'Actually it was Jehovah's Witnesses.'

'Dickhead.' She raised her eyebrows. 'Well?'

'Alright, and don't laugh. No more getting hammered and no more feeling sorry for myself; I'm going to get Penny back.'

Vicky huffed. 'You're wasting your time, handsome.'

'Well at least you didn't laugh. But I've got to try. I've been a right wimp.'

'Whatever. Still it's good to see you on the up at last.

'Thanks. Look, I'm in a rush but I'd love to have a chat. If Cyril forgives me and you're not busy, fancy a drink later?'

'What have you done now?'

'I chucked up on his floor last night, apparently.'

'Oh dear, that wasn't very clever. If Cyril's dog hasn't eaten you, seven-thirty?'

'Great. Seven-thirty it is.'

She went to walk away but turned back. 'It's weird meeting you now, Tom. I've been thinking about giving you a bell.'

'Yeah, what about?'

She shrugged. 'Oh, nothing much – catch up sort of thing. We'll chat later.'

Tommy felt a glow inside when she pecked him on the cheek and walked away. The feeling vanished when he saw the pub at the end of the street.

The Who'd a Thot It, by any standard, was a dive. But for all his bark, Cyril rarely bit. Tommy liked Cyril. Cyril seemed to like him. There was the outside chance that an apology would be greeted by an encounter with Buster the

Rottweiler. But it was an outside chance.

With the words 'faint heart never won fair lady' repeating in his head, he walked towards the next tick on the list.

DAGGERS IN THEIR SMILES

MONDAY EVENING, QUEENSWAY, WEST LONDON, SEVEN-THIRTY

'Thanks again, Cyril,' said Tommy, collecting the change and pocketing it. 'Never again, I promise.'

'You don't need to keep saying it, Tommy boy. I got my twenty back and it's good to see you making an effort at last.' He winked. 'Just remember Buster isn't as forgiving as I am.'

'Right, thanks, you're a top man, Cyril.'

'You sure you don't want the Cornish pasty?'

'No thanks.' Tommy's olfactory memory churned his stomach. 'The cheese roll will be fine.'

He picked up the roll and drinks but hesitated. 'Do you have any idea where that old fellow lives?'

'What old fellow?'

'Ollie – the one I was drinking with.'

'No. Never clapped eyes on him before last night'

'What about this morning, when he left the money, didn't he say anything?'

'I never saw him. Found a note on the bar with the twenty underneath.' Cyril's brow creased. 'Strange thing was he had beautiful handwriting for an old drunk.'

Tommy was intrigued. 'What did the note say?'

'The note? Not much. *Mission accomplished, kind regards, Ollie A.*'

'Can I see it?'

'I chucked it in the bin.'

'That's a shame. If he does come in again—'

'I'll let you know.'

He left to serve another customer.

*

'Is it a good job, Tom?' said Vicky as he placed the drinks on the table.

'Mm?' He was thinking about Ollie.

She poked him in the ribs. 'Is the job any good?'

'Sorry, yeah, it's not bad.' Ollie A., he thought. Wonder what the *A* stands for?

'Ahem. I'm here,' she said sternly. 'Focus on me.'

'Right, sorry. I'll be working from home on the computer, proof reading. Old Bingham at the job centre pulled a few strings with a mate at Fodder and Stilton, a publisher. Kind of up my alley really, and the money's reasonable.

'Like you need the cash. Why not forget the job and Penny and whisk me off to the Caribbean.'

'And break a thousand hearts?'

'Hundreds, Tom. Anyway, you're getting it together at long last, that's great.'

'Where would I be without you and Cyril?'

'People care about you, dickhead!'

'Sorry.'

'Say *sorry* one more time and I'll leave.' After a short silence she said, 'Are you going to ditch that crummy bed-sit now?'

He shrugged. 'Maybe – dunno. Now I've cleaned it up it's not so bad.'

She laughed. 'You're joking.'

'No I'm not. The Barbican wasn't up to much: plastic friends with daggers in their smiles, flashy restaurants and flash cars. Whatever happens, I'm not going back to that.'

'But it's better than here,' she said, taking a sip of red wine.

'It's not all it's cracked up to be, Vicky. I'd rather have what I've got now.'

'Don't be daft. If I had the choice, I'd be gone, gone, gone.'

'I'd rather have you than a hundred of that lot.'

She smiled, leaned over the table and tweaked his cheek. 'But you haven't had me, have you?'

'I don't mean that way.' he said, flustered.

One inebriated evening he'd offered her money. Her vehement refusal with the threat of never speaking to him again still smarted. She'd said, 'It'll be a cold day in hell when you become one of my customers, Tommy Boyle.'

Vicky held her smile. 'I'm only playing. I reckon we got that one straight a while back. So, give me one good reason why you'd rather have this?' She swept her arm out to indicate the threadbare pub with its motley collection of customers.

'I suppose it's because these are real people, not all puffed up like that lot I used to mix with. And another thing, I get loads of inspiration for my writing, you know, characters. Take my landlord and Sven Cheesewright for instance; you couldn't invent them if you tried.'

'I had better not be one of your characters, Tom.'

He winked. 'I wouldn't use your real name.'

'Oh, I can see it now,' said Vicky with an airy expression, 'I'd be the inspiration for a beautiful fairy princess.' She frowned. 'I would be beautiful, wouldn't I?'

'It goes without saying.'

'Okay, so this beautiful fairy princess wins the heart of the handsome fairy prince and they live happily ever after in a fairy-tale castle, where she regularly manacles him to a bed and whips him.'

Tommy laughed.

'A bestseller?'

'You'd better give up your job and we'll write together.'

'I don't think Penny would like that.'

An unexpected wave of guilt hit Tommy and he didn't comment.

She eyed him shrewdly for a moment. 'Does winning back your love have anything to do with getting one over on the Chisholms?'

'No! No way. I just want Penny back.'

'That's a shame.' She drained her glass. 'I think I've got time for one more.'

Tommy knew he was taking some bait but couldn't resist it. 'What if it did?'

'Aha,' she said, wagging a finger. 'I mentioned earlier today I was thinking about giving you a bell, and it wasn't just to catch up. Do you know why I didn't?'

He shook his head.

'Because you wouldn't have known what to do with what I'm going to tell you, that's why. You would have screwed up and made a drunken prat of yourself.'

Tommy shook his head again.

'But you have changed, Tom – I can see it in your eyes. I reckon the brain has finally engaged at last. You're wasting your time with Penny, though.'

'Hold on a minute–'

'Let me finish. But those guys set you up and – well, what goes around comes around. Get me another.'

Tommy prised himself away and quickly returned with a glass of wine.

'Okay, fasten your seat belt,' said Vicky. 'But remember, if it had been one of *my* clients you'd never hear this story. Confidentiality is one reason why I get top dollar. However, some of my colleagues don't share the same work ethic. Maybe I'll break that rule when you write my memoirs one day, but until then I haven't said a word – got it?'

Tommy nodded.

'Well, a friend of mine got a call a few weeks back. A

cab collected her and took her to the High Tower Hotel. She said it was one of the strangest visits she'd had, not nasty stuff, just weird. In the penthouse suite this well-spoken man opened a suitcase and pulled out some clothes. He asked her to strip off and dress up as Napoleon. Then he pulls up some marching band on a smart phone, puts on a big hat with a feather in it and... Well, the in and outs aren't important.'

Tommy laughed. 'See what I mean about characters? Plenty of material there for my book.' Vicky's serious expression cut short his laughter.

'You may want to do more than use it in your book, Tom. The guy didn't give a name, obviously, but when he's cleaning up in the bathroom my indiscreet friend checked out his jacket pocket.' She took a deep breath. 'You ready for this?'

The pub seemed to have become deathly silent and Vicky the only person in the room apart from him.

'His name was Hector Chisholm.'

Tommy fell back in his chair. He mouthed a few words but all that came out was, 'Gonzo?'

'No, this was Sir Hector Chisholm – junior's old man.' Her dark eyes sparkled. 'My friend need never know, but you do, so make good use of it and don't screw up.'

PIE-EYED
WEDNESDAY LUNCHTIME, BIGGIN HILL

Nestat woke, bound and gagged, to a falsetto voice singing 'Everybody loves somebody sometimes'.

Waking up in strange places was becoming tiresome, if routine. He was lying on something hard and was naked – naked! That was new. The last conscious seconds in the toilet filtered back. They had been gassed, but by whom?

The singing voice changed tunes: something by Rodgers and Hammerstein where all the notes had been shifted slightly to the left, and some removed.

Nestat's worst fears possessed him: was he in the lair of an assassin with access to the Shopping List, looking for a payday?

Experience told him not to let his captor know he was awake. The bonds felt tight. Not good. Eyes closed, he used his finely-honed senses to survey the locale, to find anything that might give him some advantage.

The smell of cooking was intense: buttery pastry, stewed meat with onions. One of the pie factories, perhaps? He hadn't travelled far, then. Another aroma, subliminal, and to the untrained nose indiscernible, caught his attention. For a moment it defied him, the way a '67

Grand Cru Saint-Emilion had when determining who picked the grape and at what time of the day the press had occurred. But he'd got the answer then and he'd get it now. His twitching nostrils didn't let him down. Sawdust and something else – blood? *Sawdust and blood?*

Opening his eyes he saw a thin, middle-aged man with a bouffant hairstyle. He wore floral rubber trousers and matching top and was busily putting an edge on a large meat cleaver.

'Hello, sleepy head,' he said in a camp voice, placing the blade on a wooden chopping block. 'Who've been naughty boys then?'

Nestat turned to see Hal, also bound and gagged, lying supine on a heavy duty, wooden butcher's table.

'Oh yes, I got the call ten minutes ago, adding your big friend to the list.'

Nestat faced his captor. The man leant over him and checked the ropes for tightness. 'I hope you don't mind me leaving the gag on – can't stand chatterboxes when I'm working.'

Nestat recognised the face from somewhere, some long-closed file.

'Let me introduce myself, I'm Barry Stodey, pie manufacturing and distribution. Julian Wend is my partner and oversees our national chain of gentlemen's hairdressing salons. You're in a production line, Agent Montgomery.'

Nestat's eyes widened.

'But I'm having a teensy weenie little problem working out where to place you, once you're processed that is.'

Nestat couldn't get his eyes any wider, but he tried.

'You see, my clever, handsome man, your halcyon days at Eton ...' He stopped and uttered a high-pitched laugh, forced from his lungs like meat through a mincer. 'Ha ha ha ha. Eton. Eton. How queer. You went to Eton and you are going to be *eaten*. How delicious. Ha ha ha ha. What's the matter? You don't find it funny?'

As best he could, through his gag, Nestat said, 'hirarious'.

Stodey ran his rubber-gloved hand along Nestat's cheek, then turned abruptly and recommenced sharpening the cleaver.

'So, your days in Eton would put you into the Pies R Us category.' Satisfied by the edge on the blade, he placed the cleaver into a kind of utility belt, on which hung various tools of evisceration. 'Then again, I could loosely slip you into Shepherd's Pie International as you attended Oxford University and the surrounding hills have sheep and shepherds on them – well, I think they still do? They did in Vaughn Williams' *Oxford Elegy*. I love Vaughn Williams, don't you? Oh, and Iggy Pop. Where was I? Ah yes. You were born in Scotland so Scots Pie Distribution UK is certainly an option. You see, poppet, *you're* a bit tricky.' Stodey's eyes strayed to Nestat's groin. 'But I know exactly what to do with that morsel. It's lunchtime.'

Nestat watched with horror as Stodey withdrew the cleaver from his belt. He struggled and twisted, but the bonds held firm.

'I'll gig you ore unny dan dem,' he offered.

'Suffering from a spot of indigestion, are we,' said Stodey with mock concern. 'That'll soon pass when I rip out your stomach and bowels – and you will be awake when I do, believe me. But all in good time, let's start with lunch.' Stodey slammed the blade into the table an inch from his head. 'And of course there is your friend there with the boggle eyes. Does he have mental health issues?'

Nestat turned his head to see Hal awake and staring about wild-eyed. As a Special Agent he had been trained to accept a nasty end might come one day, and it looked like the day had come. But this wasn't a bullet to the head, quick and relatively painless like Margot's could have been, no, this was going to be off-the-scale excruciatingly painful. His tongue probed the rear molar containing cyanide. His thoughts went out to Hal, the gentle giant:

what must be going through *his* mind? As a non-field agent, Nestat doubted Hal possessed a deadly rear tooth to cut short the agony; every cut would be horribly painful.

'I've had a brainwave,' said Stodey with excitement. 'I'll mix you both up in all the pies. You'll be a pie to die for. Or is it to die for a pie?' He sniggered nasally and yanked the cleaver from the table.

Nestat closed his eyes, pushed a little harder on the tooth and waited for the moment when the blade made contact with his unmentionables. That would be the point of no return, when he would lever the tooth out with his tongue and set off the miniature explosive, releasing the cyanide. Not for the first time, he felt the peaceful acceptance of death melt his worries. Not for the first time, death decided not to come.

A roar like an enraged bull. A frightened squeak. Opening one eye, he saw Hal chasing Stodey around the room, and Hal had the cleaver. A quick glance at the table alongside revealed the ropes frayed and broken as if torn apart by incredible strength.

Eyes wide open now and with his tongue in full retreat from the deadly tooth, Nestat watched as they dodged and ducked, until finally Stodey tripped and fell behind a table. Hal jumped on him, and although out of sight, Nestat saw the big man's arm raised high, the cleaver in hand. It rose and fell many times.

Hal stood, naked, spattered in blood, his expression murderous and cruel, just like in the hotel room. In one hand he held the cleaver, in the other, Barry Stodey's dripping head.

He roared, 'I am Halgoth, Warlord of the Beordeed and Master of the Haegarand!' and fell to the floor in a heap.

*

Using the Kniphausen technique it still took Nestat five minutes to loosen the rope enough to free his hands, during which time Hal's large snoring frame hadn't moved.

He found his gun, Hal's rucksack and their clothes in a large bin liner under a table. Once dressed, and horrified at the condition of his attire, he gave full attention to the big man on the floor, whose expression resembled a contented, sleeping child cuddling a teddy bear, only this comforter had bug eyes, a terrified expression and bouffant hair style.

It crossed Nestat's mind to leave him and make off. But the man had saved his life – twice; he owed him that. Whoever or whatever he was.

Easing the severed head out of Hal's grasp, he placed it next to Stodey's body on the sawdust-covered floor. Someone was bound to come soon, the Shopping List guaranteed that, so getting Hal sorted and both of them away was paramount, speed was of the essence.

He filled a bucket with water from a large ceramic sink and threw the contents over the snoring hulk.

'Flippin' heck, wow, what happened?' said Hal, leaping unsteadily to his feet. 'Where am I? Shit! I've got no clothes on.'

'Clean up, get dressed in double time and let's get out of here,' said Nestat dumping Hal's clothes and a towel on the table.

'Ye Gods!' screamed Hal looking at his hands. 'Is this blood?'

'Yes, but not yours. Come on, we've got to go.'

Hal looked terrified. 'What happened?'

'You don't remember?'

'Being in the toilet and... and... no.'

'Never mind,' said Nestat. 'I'll fill you in when we're out of here. But just to help you get a move on, they've put you on the Shopping List.'

Within fifteen minutes they had made their escape and were in a cab heading back into London and Knightsbridge.

*

Looking like a shaggy dog, Hal aimlessly fiddled with his

rucksack; he mumbled, 'How many times?'

'Six or seven, maybe ten, really hard blows. Obviously the cleaver wasn't as sharp as I thought.' Nestat didn't look at Hal but stared out the cab window into the streets of London, scanning faces, assessing threats. 'And you called yourself something.'

'Something?'

'Yes – Master of the Beordeed, or something.'

'Master of the Haegarand?'

'Yes, something like that.' Nestat faced Hal. 'You appear to have multiple personalities, my friend, multiple *useful* personalities.'

'I had a vision, while I was out.'

'Wonderful,' said Nestat, turning back to the window, 'you must tell me about it someday.'

'She's on a plane, I saw it,' said Hal quietly.

Nestat nodded. 'Did you see anything else: where the plane was going, other people with her, that sort of thing?'

'No.' Hal bowed his head.

'She was in Biggin Hill, Hal. Why else would she go there unless it was to get on a plane? Tell me something I don't know already.'

'Maybe she sent another signal.'

Hal opened the rucksack, rummaged about and pulled out a GPS tracker. He tapped keys and text flew up the screen. 'I was right. It's faint but it is definitely from her, another signal. It came from somewhere near Whitehaven.'

Nestat became attentive. 'Whitehaven in Cumbria?'

'Yeah. Why is she sending us to her apartment when the plane is near Whitehaven?'

The cab rumbled to stop.

Nestat opened his door. 'Let's find out, shall we? I'm pretty certain I know what I'm looking for, but I wish it wasn't in Margot's flat.'

'Why?'

'An eagle always guards its nest, Hal, and Margot is a very dangerous bird. Getting in alive is going to be tricky.

Getting out alive, even trickier.'

ASSEMBLING THE CAST
MONDAY NIGHT, NOTTING HILL

In the wake of Vicky's bombshell, the first inkling of a plan had begun to materialise in Tommy's head on the tube journey home, just threads here and there, but something. Consumed by his thoughts, he almost forgot the meaty promise to Mr Viscotti. He didn't, however, forget Viscotti's shady brothers as they were a potential thread in the revenge tapestry taking shape, and it was this that prompted a call to the 24-hour supermarket for the steak.

*

'Thank-a-you,' said Viscotti, taking the parcel from Tommy. 'You're a good boy. 'I'll check about the other thing, okay.'

Tommy clapped his hands together when Viscotti's door closed. The chase was afoot, and yet the smile he carried all the way to the bedsit faded as he slammed home the deadbolt; exhaustion and a thumping head from the previous night's overindulgence finally overcame him. Downing a couple of painkillers, he threw himself on the sofa-bed.

After half an hour tossing and turning, he gave up

trying to sleep and got up to flick the kettle on for a cup of coffee. A drink of something stronger was tempting, but he resisted.

Mug in hand, he went to the small desk under the only window and opened his laptop. As a concert pianist might, he raised his hands then launched onto the keys, into his work, tap-tapping out the stories, pouring his beautiful mind into the screen.

Three hours later and with the untouched coffee stone cold, he shut the lid, sat back and smiled. 'I think I might have something there.'

Stretching, he stood and went to the phone by the front door. A glance at his watch showed two-thirty in the morning. Only two people he knew would be up and about at this time. He picked up the phone and dialled.

It rang to the point where a voice message was imminent, but then Sven Cheesewright answered.

'Yo, Tommy. Hold on a mo – it went that way, towards the runway – how's tricks, buddy – no, that way!'

Tommy held the phone away from his ear. A siren blared then faded fast. 'Sven, what's happening; where are you?'

'Heathrow airport. Hold on a sec, Tom. The other one's in the canal.'

The siren was distant now and Tommy heard a muffled but irate voice with whom Sven was obviously conversing.

'Yeah, that's right, the canal.'

Muffled voice.

'Look, it's not my fault.'

Muffled voice.

'And the same to you, I wouldn't help again if you begged me.'

Tommy heard boots crunching over gravel, the solid slam of Sven's truck door and then some quietly uttered Swedish profanities.

'Sorry about that. Bloody llamas.'

'Llamas?' echoed Tommy.

'I had to pick up a couple of llamas from airline cargo and deliver them to the quarantine centre on the edge of the airport.'

'I didn't know they flew things like that about?'

'You'd be amazed, Tom. I've carted bulls, Lamborghinis, live lobsters and dead bodies to name a few. First time I've done llamas, though. It'll be the last, I can tell you. The buggers spit, did you know that?'

'No I didn't. So what happened?'

'They wouldn't come out of the crate. These vets or whatever they are were faffing about for ages, but they wouldn't budge. Time is money for me, Tom, so I stepped in and helped.'

Tommy's face screwed up as he covered the mouth piece and silently laughed.

'Took off my fluorescent jacket and waved it in their faces. That's when one spat at me, but it got the buggers moving all right – a kind of stampede. The stupid vets jumped out the way, the llamas barged through the gate and legged it.'

Tommy heard another siren in the background, 'It doesn't sound like your fault, Sven.'

'Nah, but I bet I'll get a bollocking. One guy said they'd have to close a runway if they're not rounded up before morning. Anyway, what you phoning me for at – shit, this time?'

'Can you call round tomorrow, Sven, once you're up and about? I need your help.'

'Sure. What's cooking?'

'A bit of private detective work.' Tommy knew this would get him wriggling with excitement. Sven was a fan of every gangster and black and white gumshoe movie ever made, to the point where he sometimes mixed up reality with fiction.

'You bet, Tom. I can come round first thing if you like?'

'No, get your beauty sleep. After lunch will be fine.'

'Can you give me a side order on the main course?'

Tommy smiled; Sven was already slipping badly into character. 'You keep this to yourself, okay.'

'Mum's the word.'

Tommy laid it on. 'It involves the Chisholms. It's payback time, Sven, and I'm playing hardball.'

'Like it, Tom, like it. You don't sound pissed, by the way?'

'That's all over. You're going to meet a different Thomas Boyle tomorrow, no more booze, so be prepared.'

'Great, looking forward to it – shame about the booze, though.'

'Goodnight, Sven, and all the best with the llamas.'

Tommy hung up and took a moment to collate everything. Surprisingly, and without prompting, Vicky had offered to help if she could; he'd call her first thing. He had reminded Viscotti of his offer when dropping off the steak and had got an affirmative. A visit in the morning would get the wheels turning. Sven was primed and ready to go, which only left Penny. A phone call wasn't going to be so easy without Gonzo getting wind of it so he decided to catch her before she went into work; to let her see the new Tommy in the flesh, to know he meant business. If there *were* any plot holes they would have to be ironed out as things went along. He concluded his thoughts feeling vaguely on top of things for the first time in months. Setting the alarm for six-thirty, he climbed under the duvet and fell asleep in seconds.

BRIEF ENCOUNTER
TUESDAY MORNING, NOTTING HILL

The alarm dragged Tommy from pleasant dreams into the pathetic excuse for a shower, where he took fifteen minutes struggling to wash under a warm dribble of water.

'You need a prostate operation,' he muttered at the shower head, rinsing the last vestiges of shampoo from his hair. Vicky's words the previous night came back to him, about ditching the bed-sit, she was right. It *was* crummy. It might suit some writers but not this one.

He shaved and dressed smartly, grabbed some keys from a wall rack by the phone and left.

Hailing a cab outside, he climbed in and gave the driver the address. A quick check of the watch, seven-thirty, confirmed he was running on time.

Fifteen minutes later, the cab cut back into heavy traffic, leaving him standing next to Salisbury Mews. Pulling keys from his pocket, he walked into the cobbled street, stopping in front of a garage door.

He paused a moment. On the other side of the door sat an object that represented the world he had once lived in. Taking a deep breath, he unlocked the up-and-over door and yanked it open, revealing a dustsheet-covered car.

Giving it a slight tug, the lightweight material slid gently over the burnished paint and fell to the ground. Before him stood an Audi RS5. He pressed the remote but nothing happened.

Tommy knew pretty much everything about the trading floor, but cars he didn't know. Makes and models yes, he knew those because they reflected status, but what went on under the bonnet was a mystery, which he proved when manually unlocking the door and trying to start the engine.

'Bollocks! Why haven't all the lights come on?'

The answer to his question came from a man poking his head round the door of the garage, mouthing words and waving.

The electric windows didn't work either.

'Why aren't you working?' He got out of the car.

'Your battery is flat,' said the man.

'Is it? Damn!'

'I saw you arrive from my kitchen window.'

'Right,' said Tommy vaguely.

I'm Rodger Smythe – number eight? How are you, Mr Boyle.'

'Do I know you?'

'You rent the garage from me, remember?'

He didn't remember. He checked his watch and groaned. 'Oh no.'

'Would you like me to arrange for a mechanic to call?' said Smythe.

'That's very kind but I'm running late.' Leaving the car door open, he walked briskly out of the garage.

'It's really not a problem,' said Smythe with a friendly smile. 'We can sort out the bill later.'

'Alright then, thanks. Can you do me a favour and lock up, please?

'Certainly.'

'And you can sell it for me if you like,' Tommy added. 'Take a few grand for yourself.'

'Are you serious?'

'Yeah,' he said walking away. 'The keys are in it. Give me a call.'

He didn't hear what Smythe said as he broke into a trot towards the main road; the day was off to a bad start.

*

Tommy saw Penny only fifty yards from the entrance to *Harrison and Chipley Chartered Accountants, Fulham Road*, her place of work.

'Stop here,' he said, pushing two twenties through the cab partition.

'Right ho, mate,' said the cab driver cheerily as he screeched to a halt.

Ignoring his thanks, Tommy leapt out and ran. 'Penny! Penny!'

She turned, looked about, saw him and appeared to panic.

'It's important, Penny, I'm not drunk.'

She seemed about to make a dash for the building. He understood because when someone surprises you and shouts 'I'm not drunk!' they usually are. She hesitated, giving him enough time to reach her.

'Just a few minutes, Penny, please? It really is very important.'

'Tommy, what is it now,' she said with a touch of anger as he stopped in front of her.

Taking a second to catch his breath, it hit him how out of condition he was. Gym would be added to the list. Sweating and gasping, he didn't project the cool and collected image he had planned. Could he salvage the situation? 'I'm sorry. I wanted to pick you up outside the station but the car wouldn't start.'

'You were going to drive?' she said surprised.

'I'm stone cold sober. I meant what I said yesterday on the phone.'

'I'm glad to hear it. You gave me a scare with that 'going to do myself in' trick.'

'Right.' He didn't think it wise to tell her the truth, that there was no *trick*. 'I also meant what I said about winning you back.'

She closed her eyes for a second then said with a weary sadness, 'A lot has happened, Tommy. It's not the same anymore. The fact you mentioned suicide shows this has become abnormal.'

'Yeah, I know. I was stupid. But you think I'm a cheat and a liar. What if I were to prove otherwise?'

'Didn't you have the chance to do that months ago? The FSA found you guilty. You were lucky the prosecution fell through.'

'I was set up, Penny. I didn't have a leg to stand on.' He stared at his feet for a second then looked at her, finding it difficult not to sound bitter when he said, 'It didn't help you going off with Chisholm; that took the fight out of me.'

Penny's brow furrowed. 'I stuck with you for months, permanently drunk and feeling sorry for yourself, even when you moved into that dreadful bed-sit. I didn't just dump you, Tommy. If it hadn't been for Hector I would've had a nervous breakdown.'

'I know, Penny, and I'm really sorry,' he said glumly. 'I've been such a wimp.' He brightened. 'But something has come up and I've got the chance to prove my innocence.'

'That's great, but I can't stand talking all day; I'm going to be late.'

'I want you to hear it, Penny – first-hand.'

'What?'

'Don't worry, you won't be involved. All you'll have to do is listen in to a conversation.'

'This is mad, Tommy. I've got to go.' She turned to walk away.

Desperation and anger welled up in him. 'Didn't I mean anything to you? Isn't it important I clear my name?'

She stopped and looked at him. 'Of course, but–'

'Then help me. I need a witness, and it has to be you.

Give me this one last chance, *please?*'

She looked at him keenly. 'This doesn't involve Hector, does it?'

'Gonzo? Sorry. No, it doesn't involve him.'

She sighed. 'I can't believe I'm doing this. What will I have to do?'

'It'll be a meeting one evening – tomorrow or the next day. I don't know where and what time exactly, but I'll call you when I do.'

'It all sounds very vague, Tommy.'

'Yeah, I know it does at the moment. But getting someone important to admit I was innocent, and I mean the one person who can clear my name, isn't an easy thing to organise. Please bear with me. You must see how important this is?'

She took a moment to think. 'Okay, but don't you dare call me at the house. Hector was close to reporting you to the police the other morning.'

'Was he?' Tommy suppressed the urge to call him a bastard. 'I'll call your mobile then.'

'I have a new number. Hector organised it.'

'Did he?' Tommy sensed another tenuous thread snapping in their relationship. 'Can I have it? I'll never call on it again afterwards, I promise.'

She nodded reluctantly and gave him the number. 'I can't make it tomorrow but I can on Thursday; Hector is at his club until late that day. After that it'll be equally impossible until next week.'

'Right, it'll have to be Thursday then. Thanks, Penny, this means a great deal to me. And, eh, don't mention anything to Hector, will you.'

'If he knew I was going to meet you he'd hit the roof. This is a one-off, Tommy. I hope it all works out for you.'

'You'll see. I'm not the bad guy. Maybe then we can–'

She cut across him. 'I have to go now.'

He received her cursory peck on the cheek. No warmth.

'Bye, Penny. And thanks again.'

She walked away quickly.

The meeting hadn't gone the way he wanted, but she had at least agreed to be present. He had to see Vicky, Sven and the Viscotti brothers today, and only after these elements had been secured could everything go ahead. A lot of assumptions and some calculated guesswork were involved, but he hadn't been a top trader for nothing. It had to work.

GONE FISHING
WEDNESDAY AFTERNOON, KNIGHTSBRIDGE

Nestat and Hal stepped out of the lift onto deep-pile, crimson carpet. Along the corridor were two doors on each side. Nestat stopped before a heavy mahogany door, apartment nine.

'This is it, Hal.'

The big man's brow creased. 'There's nobody in, is there? I mean, she's on a plane. Don't you have a key?'

'I don't, but I know where to find one. Stay put and keep clear of the spy-hole.'

Nestat walked to the far end of the corridor where an oil painting of the second battle of Chattanooga hung on the wall above a small table bearing a vase of flowers. Reaching up, he felt behind the gilt frame and removed a key held in place by a piece of blue-tack. Peeling it away, he returned to Hal and stuck the blob on the spy-hole. The sound of a latch clicking home on the other side of the door followed.

'Okay, one down,' said Nestat, inserting the key into the lock. 'Let's hope I've got this right – twelve degrees anti-clockwise, sixteen degrees clockwise.' Pausing a moment, he twisted the ornate brass knob and the door opened with a gentle push. Staying on the threshold, he reached in and flicked a switch on the wall inside. The sound of another latch locking into place followed.

'Okay, I reckon it's safe to go into the hall now.'

Hal glanced about as they walked in. 'The lady has good taste. Some of this stuff must be worth a fortune.' He nudged Nestat. 'There's a photo of you on the sideboard.'

Nestat picked up the silver framed photo. 'Strange, I've never noticed this before. It was taken at a Savoy charity dinner in support of stamping out rickets in Chelsea. I'm surprised she kept it, let alone had it framed.'

'Maybe she fancies you?'

'Fancies me? She adored me.' Nestat heard his own words before he knew what he was saying. He silenced his thoughts and raised a finger to his lips for quiet.

'There,' he whispered. 'See that.'

A camera was tracing their path across the entrance hall. A sawn-off shotgun, stuck limpet-like to the device was also following their progress.

Hal gulped.

Nestat tip-toed over to a mirror at the end of the hall. Beside it, on a marble plinth, a semi-naked statue of Mae West smirked sexily. He twisted her art-deco nipple. The camera whined and then pointed submissively downwards while the mirror swung back revealing a set of diamante-encrusted shuriken in a clay-pigeon trap.

'If I hadn't disarmed the trigger mechanism these would have greeted us when we stepped over the threshold.'

Hal stepped sideways out of the line of fire and placed a hand on a rococo sideboard.

'Freeze!'

'W-W-What is it now?' said Hal

'Keep perfectly still.'

Without moving his head, the big man looked down and saw a large spider rearing up into attack stance. It leapt onto the back of his hand. He screamed.

In the blink of an eye, Nestat slipped out his Budleigh Salterton mini throwing dagger set, selected one and threw. The knife swept the spider off Hal's hand, pinning it to the wall below a portrait of Margaret Thatcher wearing a fedora.

'A Brazilian Wandering Spider, Hal,' said Nestat. 'Quite lethal.'

'What else is here? What's next? No, don't tell me. Just don't let me die.'

'I'll do my best. I'll lead and you follow, okay?'

'You bet.'

'Right, onto the kitchen. Let's get what we're looking for and leave.'

'But, what *are* we looking for?'

'You'll see – I hope.'

Nestat went to a closed door, stretched up and pressed the eye-patch on a photograph of Moshe Dyane hanging above the lintel. A sharp click unlatched something, followed by an electric motor running for a few seconds. He opened the door.

He saw it immediately on the large permafrost fridge freezer, a magnet in mock-metallic plastic bearing a coat of arms above a cow and bicycle. Beneath the motif, in worn, gilt letters, were the words, *Welcome to Milton Keynes, Less Mediocre Than You Think!* The magnet held a business card. He smiled.

'Oh dear,' he said, the smile fading.

'What's up?' said Hal.

'The floor, it's a maze of pressure pads and explosives.'

'So switch them off.'

'Ah, yes. That would be sensible. Thing is, I don't know how. I'm not really a kitchen person. She did tell me once how to disarm it but I may have been distracted. I find it difficult to assimilate information when I'm naked.'

Remaining on the threshold, Nestat reached in and checked the walls but found nothing. 'Damn it! I don't know where the switch is.'

'It all looks okay,' said Hal.

'Do *you* want to walk over and get that business card; it's under the fridge magnet?'

'Is that what we're after, a business card?'

'Yes. Off you go. I'll wait here.'

Hal didn't move.

'Right, I thought not.' Nestat faced the fridge once more. 'Only one thing for it, lightning speed and fingers crossed.'

Everything appeared innocuous, and it was this that caused a bead of sweat to break out on Nestat's brow. 'I'm off on the count of three. Got a medic-kit in that knapsack of yours, Hal: tourniquets, a defibrillator, morphine?'

'No. Sorry. Hold on a minute, though.' He rummaged, muttering, 'Night vision binoculars, ectoplasm burns kit, cosmic energy detector. Aha, here it is – Savlon!'

A flicker of a smile cracked Nestat's grim expression. He took a deep breath. 'Here I go then. One. Two. Three.'

He covered the distance to the fridge in four gymnastic flips. Tearing the card from beneath the magnet, he spun to commence the return journey. Keeping his eyes fixed on Hal at the door, he didn't notice the kitchen spring into life at first, but the big man's dismayed expression triggered survival mode.

Time slowed. A razor-edged wall-clock spun past his face, a hair's breadth in front of his eyes. Nestat launched into a series of balletic somersaults, touching the sensitive floor pads with the grace and lightness of a small child. Mid-spin, he remembered the advice that Baryshnikov had given him in the Agency Ballet Corps – 'Always smile!' That advice seemed strangely irrelevant now as the pressure-pad black tiles began to flash red and a voice signalled a countdown that started from two. Shaken, and slightly stirred, he landed on his haunches in front of Hal.

The room exploded.

*

Rising to his feet, Nestat brushed the ash from his suit and read the business card: 'Witherspoon and Smythe, haberdashers and purveyors of quality fish to Her Majesty, 42 Mount Vesuvius Street, E4.'

Hal lay on his back, covered in debris. He sat up and shook his head in disbelief

Nestat winked. 'You can put away the Savlon now.'

*

Somehow, the establishment of Witherspoon and Smythe had managed to escape the developers in their quest to eradicate every last trace of London slums. The old-curiosity-shop of a building, sandwiched between concrete and glass office blocks, stood out like a beggar at the Barbican.

'This can't be the place,' said Hal, getting out of the cab.

'Keep the change,' said Nestat handing some notes to the cabby. 'Stay nearby and there's another fifty on your fare when we've finished our business.'

He turned to Hal. 'That's what's on the card. Part of the crumb trail.'

They walked over to the shop. Behind the grimy window a huge, stuffed moray eel stared at them. Above the savage fish, suspended on wires, hung a collection of the more bizarre species of sea-life inhabiting the ocean.

'I love fish,' said Hal, 'but do people actually eat those... whatever they are?'

'Apparently Her Majesty does – the Japanese as well, no doubt.'

Nestat turned the wrought iron handle. The door swung in to the tinkling of a bell.

The smell hit them: mothballs and fish. On the wall, behind a wooden counter, hung an icon of a haloed, female Saint holding a cod. More odd-looking stuffed fish hung on wires from the ceiling. On the linoleum floor beneath these piscine mobiles sat white freezer chests, racks with various types of cloth hung over them and everything a seamstress could ever want. On a table of its own stood an incongruity to surpass all else, a papier-mâché model of a volcano.

'Good day gentlemen.'

The greeting came from a tall, emaciated man in an ill-fitting dark suit. He had silently appeared from the shadows. Below his oiled, black hair, parted in the middle, a grey complexion supported a beak-like nose, a pencil moustache and predatory eyes. He seemed to be attempting a smile by way of a one-sided, upward twitch of his mouth.

'Am I addressing Mr. Witherspoon or Mr. Smythe,' said Nestat.

'Heimlich Smythe, sir, at your service.' He beckoned the two men over to the counter. 'Please, don't be shy. I won't bite.'

Smythe snapped his teeth together and followed with a neighing laugh. 'Now, what can I do for you fine gentlemen, mmm? Turbot perhaps, nice succulent fillets of sturgeon? Or would you prefer to browse our list of more exotic aquatic provender? Then again, mayhap a simple needle and thread, mmm?'

'Does the name Margo De Witte mean anything to you?' said Nestat.

Smythe caressed his bony chin with long fingers. 'Margot De Witte, De Witte de Margot. Nooo. The name doesn't stir any memories.' His eyes lit up. 'It's not a newly discovered fish, is it?'

Nestat took a long shot. 'How about Dr Wilberforce Slash?'

Smythe took a little jump backwards and hurriedly checked his watch. 'Ooo, is that the time? I have a basking shark to eviscerate and trousers to sew – big order. I must ask you to leave, gentlemen.' He came out from behind the counter and began ushering them towards the door.

'That'll do,' said Nestat, standing his ground. He pushed Smythe backwards towards the counter. 'What are you scared of, Smythe? How do you know Slash? Tell me everything or I'll–'

'Or you'll vot?' came a voice from the shadows. The trumpet barrel of a blunderbuss emerged, followed by an even more unpleasant looking character than Smythe. Dressed in what appeared to be a Waffen SS uniform stripped of regalia, the grossly overweight, bald and aged man kept the gun trained on Nestat and Hal.

Smythe backed away towards his colleague. 'Oh, Reinhart, they know about The Doctor.'

'Shut up!'

'You must be Witherspoon then,' said Nestat. 'Odd surnames when you are obviously of Germanic stock.'

'Zat is not your business, as is the Herr Doctor. Hands up!'

Hal's arms went skyward at lightning speed, and without checking for obstacles they dislodged a large puffer fish from its wire.

Nestat noticed Witherspoon's eyes momentarily distracted as the fish teetered on its hook then fell. He'd also assessed the two characters' weaknesses, which were manifold. Remembering his days at Oxford playing for the first fifteen, he drop-kicked the spiny fish the instant it touched the floor. It hit Witherspoon in the face, forcing his blunderbuss skyward. A loud report followed and a large part of the ceiling was blown away. Nestat leapt forward amidst dust and debris, over the counter, and with a quick twist separated the fat man's head from its spinal column. Hal hadn't even had time to lower his hands.

Nestat grabbed the lapels of Smythe's jacket. 'Right, Heimlich, into the back room for a little chat. Hal. Hal!' He turned to see the big man transfixed and staring at Witherspoon.

'Is he?' said Hal, pointing.

'Having a nap? Yes he is. Now come on. He'll come to in a few hours.'

Nestat heard Hal's heavy tread following as he

manhandled Smythe through a door and into the next room. It was quite unlike the crusty old shop: stainless steel, fluorescent lighting and white, spotless walls.

Between sobs, Smythe said, 'Is Reinhart really unconscious. I heard a crack.'

'It was only the starch in his collar,' Nestat lied, smiling weakly at Hal.

'Really?' said Hal, perking up.

'Yes, really. Now stand by the door and make sure this joker doesn't bolt. Got it?'

Hal complied and blocked the exit with his large frame.

Nestat turned on Smythe. 'Now tell me everything, or I'll pop next door and finish the job.'

Smythe sat back on a stool, his tear-stained face and sagging body signalling utter defeat. 'We designed and built his secret headquarters five years ago – a very awkward and unpleasant customer. He appeared to be falling to bits. Anyway, I told him his budget didn't run to damp-proofing, but he wouldn't have it. We have a reputation to uphold, therefore Reinhart sent a team but they never reported back. After a series of threatening letters everything went silent. That's all I know.'

'You design and build secret headquarters?' said Nestat, incredulously.

Smythe reached into a top pocket, produced a card and handed it over.

It read, 'Hockenstein bespoke off-plan secret headquarters for the evil genius, generally despotic and crazed aristocracy.' He raised an eyebrow. 'No mention of fish to Her Majesty.'

'Well we could hardly advertise the true nature of our business, could we?' said Smythe haughtily.

'But fish and haberdashery?' Nestat shook his head. 'Oh never mind. Just tell me where Slash has his headquarters.'

'We built it beneath a derelict castle in Argyllshire. Castle Montgomery, if I remember correctly.'

Nestat stumbled backwards, and it was only a stainless steel workbench that prevented him falling. He mouthed words but no sound came out. A flood of terrible memories filled his head: his father, Sally, the ridiculous Inspector Brush and the mysterious fire two days after the funeral. He'd left the castle, what was left of it, vowing never to return.

Hal abandoned his post and walked towards Nestat.

The stool spun away as Smythe seized the moment and ran for the door.

Coming to his senses, Nestat shouted, 'Stop!'

But Smythe didn't stop, even when the bullet entered his skull. His terminal velocity carried him through the door where he fell on the body of his colleague.

'I was going to shoot him anyway,' said Nestat, holstering the gun. 'Can't have them talking.'

'Them?' said Hal, his hands shaking.

'Yes, them. Witherspoon didn't have a starched collar.'

'You lied to me.'

'Yes. Yes I did. I lied and I killed two men. Welcome to the world of a field agent, Hal Goth. Now, I'm going to have a quick rummage about. Go and make sure the cab is ready when I come out.'

Hal didn't move.

Nestat's fear of returning to Castle Montgomery expressed itself as anger. 'You want that book, don't you?'

Hal nodded.

'Then go!'

With a hurt expression, Hal slouched off, leaving Nestat alone in the room.

His gut feeling had been right: Slash was behind Margot and the book. Slash would be at the end of this trail. Nestat ground his teeth as the canker of revenge ate deeper into his heart. After all these years he was going to confront the place where the nightmares began.

DOCTOR WILBERFORCE SLASH
THURSDAY, EARLY MORNING, OVER THE NORTH SEA

The airship, in stark contrast to the plane, was spacious, warm, relatively quiet and verging on luxurious. Sipping a flute of Champagne, Margot De Witte gazed out of the large window to the sea far below, rippling in a bronze tinge of first light. The white leather chair enveloped her, and Beethoven's Pastoral Symphony, playing softly in the background, gradually drained the stress of the past twenty-four hours towards her feet and the deep-pile carpet on which they rested. Apart from a visit by a blue suited attendant with the Champagne and ice bucket, she hadn't met a soul since boarding.

Her hand strayed to the outline of the small book in her clutch bag. It was safe. Anyone attempting to remove it without knowing the correct procedure would be handless and the book destroyed beyond recovery; she'd made that perfectly clear on embarkation. At the moment she held the higher ground, but unless Nestat picked up the trail she wouldn't remain there much longer.

'It's in the lap of the Gods now,' she said.

Weakened by sleep deprivation and softened by Dom Pérignon, de Witte succumbed to the soporific drone of the airship's engines and closed her eyes.

*

The laboured breathing became audible long before the source entered the spacious lounge. Opening her eyes, she turned towards the main door and saw it open a fraction and then close. Something small, dark and hairy moved quickly behind a table then remained still and out of sight. She looked at the door again as it opened fully and the unmistakable Dr. Slash entered the room.

'Margot, my dear,' he said, shuffling towards her. 'At last! I hope you are enjoying the flight?'

'Slightly more than the aeroplane, Doctor.'

'Ah, yes,' said Slash, easing into the opposite seat. 'The airship belongs to The Baron; I merely have it on lease.'

De Witte nodded and remained impassive as she struggled to hide her revulsion. Slash occupied the chair more like a pile of dirty washing than a human being. One claw of a hand slowly scratched the other beneath stained bandages, causing dandruff-like material to shed over the trouser portion of his black Lycra shell suit. The heavy platform boots, one higher than the other, looked ridiculously out of place, as did the cloak.

Slash removed his broad hat. De Witte was certain she saw something with spindly legs scuttle across his flaky scalp.

'So, where are we off to, Doctor?'

He ignored the question and fixed his eyes on her bag. 'Is it safe?'

She raised an eyebrow. 'Very. I trust the goons know what will happen if they try and tamper with it?'

'Yes, but unnecessary, Margot; we have a deal.'

'We'll have a deal when I see Father alive and well.'

'Of course, of course, The Baron is taking good care of him. When I have the book... I mean, when *The Baron* has the book, you and your father will be free to go.'

De Witte placed her hand on the bag. 'Can a mere

book be worth such effort?'

Slash's pale, bloodshot eyes betrayed a hidden fire within. She instantly appraised the reaction as hunger, a terrible, covetous hunger. But his lapse of control lasted a brief second.

'The Baron acquires many unusual items, Margot. The book is merely another curio for his collection, albeit a valuable one.'

'But he could have employed my services without kidnapping my father.'

Slash screwed up what remained of his features in an expression of reluctant resignation. 'Yes, I know, but he does like to do things his own funny way. Now, if it had been me–'

'You would have shot my mother five times in the head and dragged my father away by the hair.'

'Ah, yes, Nestat Montgomery,' said Slash, his eyes narrowing. 'You weren't so thorough there, were you, Margot?'

She felt a simultaneous wave of fear and relief grip her stomach. 'Meaning?'

'Meaning he survived. The Agency has placed him on their Shopping List; nevertheless, it was careless on your part.'

If she could have punched the air she would have, but she took a sip of Champagne instead. 'How do you know this?'

'Let's say we have our sources, Margot. But I forgive you. I made a similar mistake myself. I should have killed him those years past. But who would have thought it, mmm, that the scrawny youth would transform into such a dangerous man?'

She stared coldly ahead. 'And he is dangerous, make no mistake about that.'

'Was, Margot, was. I'm sure The Agency has it all in hand. Now! Would you care for a snack? We have some hours before docking.'

'Who's in charge of the catering, Doctor?'

He laughed, sounding like the latter stages of emphysema. 'On this occasion The Baron's chef has prepared some light meals, so no need to fret, Margot dear. My catering manager is hiding behind that table over there. Spank!'

A one-armed monkey with a small haversack on its back scampered over, jumped on the table, presented his rear end to Slash and defecated.

'You filthy little monster! There's a lady present.'

De Witte covered her nose. 'I see you're still keeping good company.'

Slash reached into the folds of the cloak and withdrew a withered monkey arm on a string. He waved it in front of Spank, who instantly fell into a submissive pose, gibbering. 'That's more like it, you little devil. If you don't behave, I'll break my promise. Now where's my snack?'

Spank opened the haversack, and after discarding numerous Snickers bar wrappers, took out a Tupperware container and handed it to Slash.

'That's more like it. Now be off with you!'

Spank repacked the bag and leapt away to the far side of the lounge.

'You must forgive my hairy friend, Margot, he forgets himself sometimes.' He pressed a red switch on the wall and placed a monogrammed, linen serviette on Spank's steamy deposit. '*Your* food will arrive in a jiffy.'

Slash leaned over the Tupperware box and, without the use of cutlery, began to eat. De Witte looked out of the window, the smell of monkey excrement and the sound of Slash feeding killed her appetite.

Less than a minute passed before a blue suit entered the room and placed a tray on a side table. Leaning out, she lifted the lid on the silver tray. The canapés looked excellent and professionally made. Selecting one, and doing her best to ignore the slobbering coming from the opposite chair, she turned her attention back to the window and the sea far below, trusting Nestat hadn't been hit and crossed off the Shopping List. Something inside told her he hadn't. The Beluga suddenly tasted good.

*

Had anyone been paying particular attention to Spank, at this very moment in time, they might have noticed his eyes narrow as he spat cherry pits onto the floor in what could be interpreted as a disdainful way. They might then have surmised that his expression was that of a monkey filled with hate and plotting revenge. But nobody was paying particular attention to Spank, at that very moment in time.

GET A GRIP
THURSDAY, ONE-THIRTY AM, ARGYLLSHIRE, SCOTLAND

Nestat leant towards the glass separating him and Hal from the cab driver. Through the windscreen ahead he saw ragged clouds racing past a Hunter's Moon, and in the distance, the outline of Castle Montgomery appearing on the skyline. He sat back heavily in the seat.

'Hal, this isn't going to be easy for me. Things happened here.'

Hal gave him a friendly pat on the arm.

Nestat didn't baulk at the gesture.

'You can stop here cabby,' said Nestat. 'What do I owe you?'

'Eight hundred and fifty quid on the meter, guv.'

Nestat opened his wallet and peeled off twenty fifty-pound notes. 'Treat yourself to a night in a hotel. May I suggest the Montgomery Arms – we passed it twenty miles ago.'

'Thanks, guv, I might just do that.'

They got out, watched the cab turn and the tail lights vanish into the night.

'I should have shot him,' said Nestat quietly, more to himself. 'It would have been a kindness.'

'How can shooting a cab driver be a kindness,' said Hal with a baffled expression.

'The Agency has found Barry Stodey and they know we're still alive. They'll track down the cab driver, find out where he took us and – bang! No loose ends, Agency policy. Alf has a wife, three kids, two greyhounds and a pigeon – seven more loose ends and seven more bangs. Leastways I could have saved his family and pets by killing him now. Get it?'

'I forgot I was on the Shopping List,' said Hal gloomily, ignoring the grim prognosis for Alf's family and pets.

'Don't ever do that, my friend. Our only hope of saving them and us is finding and killing Slash – he's responsible. I know he is. I can feel it in my gut.'

'I suppose so,' said Hal vaguely.

'Okay, have you got anything lethal in that rucksack of yours?'

'I thought you might ask something like that.' He rummaged in the bag and held out a deodorant and a cigarette lighter. 'I've seen them used as a flame thrower in movies.'

'So, we're going to attack Slash's headquarters with one gun, an aerosol of musk for men and a disposable lighter?'

Hal shrugged. 'It looked pretty lethal on the film.'

*

They made stealthily through a small copse of stunted, wind-bent trees, going prone when the castle came into full view. One hundred meters of scrub grass and thorn bushes separated them from the ancient keep and curtain walls.

'We used to play croquet on this lawn,' Nestat whispered.

'This was a lawn?'

'And mother would organise wallaby races for me and the local lads. She loved wildlife.'

'Oh – really?'

'And father would be close-by with a rifle in case things

91

got out of hand. How we laughed when he fired the odd round over our heads. You know, to spur us riders on.'

'You rode wallabies?'

'We were too young for kangaroos.'

'Eh, yes, of course you were. Look, hadn't we better–'

'Mother loved aquatic life as well. She'd spend months cruising and diving in exotic places. She had a glass-bottomed catamaran, you know. That's when the killer whale... That's... All that was left was a stiletto and... Oh hell.'

'Hey, Nestat. Pull yourself together.'

Nestat felt Hal's hand grip his arm. The instinctive desire to attack him didn't kick in, instead he wanted to confide, to feel the compassion and empathy of a friend.

He shook the hand away. 'Pass me those night-vision binos.'

Hal rummaged and handed over a pair of binoculars.

Nestat flicked a switch. They gently whirred as he surveyed the landscape.

'No razor wire. No machine gun nests. Halogen spots, but they're all broken. No concealed mini nerve gas missiles.' He lowered the binoculars. 'It's deserted. That's strange. We can't be too careful, though. Follow me.'

They crept across the open ground, Nestat vigilantly scanning left and right until they reached an arched opening that had once supported doors. They stepped over the threshold, walked through the remains of a hallway, through another door and into the roofless keep. Charred beams and piles of mouldy debris littered the weed-ridden floor.

Nestat's eyes were instantly drawn to a large fireplace at the far end of what had once been the great hall.

He pointed. 'That's where it happened, Hal.'

'You gonna be alright?'

Nestat pondered the question for a moment. For years he'd dreaded facing the demons haunting the ruined ancestral home. But a studied evaluation of the surroundings caused them to flee into the star-lit sky. Anger drove them away – anger and the desire for revenge. These emotions he *could* control. Special Agent Nestat Montgomery was in control.

'I'm fine, surprisingly. Looks like no one's at home and I'm pretty sure I know where to find the entrance to Slash's headquarters.'

'You do? Did you find some plans or something back in the shop?'

'No, but there's twisted logic in that maniac's mind. Come on.'

They made through stunted shrubs and over the rubbish to the fireplace.

'Look at the floor, Hal,' said Nestat.

'Footprints, and they're all going to and from the fire. They don't look new, though.'

'Correct. Which means?'

Hal's brow creased. 'That nobody has been here for a while?'

'That's right. It appears his headquarters have been abandoned for some time; nevertheless, we must still be very careful. Now where would the release lever to the entrance be, I wonder?'

'Why not try close to where your father was murdered.'

'Oh, Hal, when I think I nearly killed you. Good boy.'

'When did you nearly kill me?'

'It crossed my mind. Don't worry, I feel this way about most people until I get to know them.'

'Do you?'

'Yes,' said Nestat, distracted as he searched the fire surround.

One of the carved motifs appeared shinier and more worn than the rest. He grabbed it, tried a few permutations then pulled. Following a clunk and the rattling of chains, they watched the stone at the back of the hearth slowly open inwards.

Nestat drew his gun. 'Stay close.'

Bright moonlight had enabled them to find their way so far, but now they entered utter darkness: tomb-like, dank and silent, apart from dripping water.

'Break out the lights, Hal.'

Two beams of brilliant white LED light illuminated a short passageway and steps leading down. No levers, swinging pendulum blades or infrared beams, but there was a light switch, an old-fashioned Bakelite type. Hal reached over to it.

'I wouldn't bother,' said Nestat, drawing Hal's attention to a small table against the wall.

On it were piles of envelopes, all unopened. One stood out, white, with *final demand* written on it in red ink. It had been impaled with a dagger.

'He hasn't paid his electric.' Nestat winked. 'Let's go, and stay alert.'

They descended the stairs. At the base, some forty-steps down, a stone-flagged cavern opened out before them. They shone their torches around, revealing a large world map on the wall and a few workstations bearing cathode ray monitors and mouldy papers. Scattered on the floor were broken stools, Snickers bar wrappers and rusty chains. Nestat followed one chain until it ended at a set of manacles beneath a workstation.

'Looks like Slash wasn't too keen on trade unions.'

'Arrrrh!' yelled Hal.

Nestat spun round. The big man's torch pointed upward, revealing four men hanging in body shaped iron cages from the vaulted ceiling. Dressed in black overalls, their bones and tatty remnants of skin and hair made a grotesque sight, but the silicon guns jammed between their grinning teeth lifted the grim spectacle into the realms of bizarre.

'If I'm not mistaken, Witherspoon and Smythe's damp-proofing team,' said Nestat.

Leaving Hal staring at the dead men, he walked over to the map. Coloured pins were dotted about the world, but a thick red circle had been drawn on Iceland, more specifically round the volcano Eyjafjallajökull. Some words had been scrawled alongside. Nestat leant forward for closer inspection. A blob of nutty brown material obscured most of the words and all he could make out was Bo, Sheit, June 2014 and something beginning with *Zep*.

'Nestat, someone's coming,' whispered Hal

Nestat turned to see a beam of torchlight wavering in the stair passage, accompanied by shuffling feet and wheezing. He levelled the gun at the entrance into the room. Could Slash be here after all? Had everything been an elaborate trick to lure him into his clutches? Would the lights suddenly come on and reveal henchmen lurking in hidden alcoves? His eyes narrowed as a forefinger caressed the trigger.

'Who's there?' said a not unfamiliar voice. 'I'm armed.'

Hal moved over to Nestat and shuffled behind him.

The voice didn't belong to Slash. Nestat racked his brain, knowing he'd heard it before.

A shadowy figure behind the light reached the bottom of the stairs.

'One more step and I'll shoot,' said Nestat. 'Who are you?'

The light, and something else, fell to the floor. 'Master Montgomery?'

Keeping the gun steady, Nestat shone his torch on the man's face. 'Ye gods, MacGrip?'

'Oh, Master Montgomery,' said the man, tottering forward with outstretched arms. 'Can it be you've come home, at last?'

Nestat holstered the gun and went forward to meet the man, who walked straight past and flung his arms around Hal.

'Here, gerroff,' said Hal.

'I'm here, MacGrip,' said Nestat.

The two men embraced.

'My eyesight isn't what it was, Master Montgomery.

Can it be true?' He began to sob.

'What's going on?' said Hal.

'This is our faithful retainer,' said Nestat, holding the embrace and gently patting the man's back. 'I though he was dead.' He slowly pushed the old man away to hold him at arm's length. 'I thought you were dead, MacGrip – in the fire. What happened?'

'Oh that terrible night of the fire, Master Montgomery. The lines were down because of the terrible storm the night before. I went to phone the fire brigade in the village. It was... was...'

'Terrible?' Nestat volunteered.

'That's it, terrible.'

'But I never saw you again, MacGrip. I stayed in the village for a couple of weeks after the fire before heading off to Oxford.'

'I got lost and found myself on the beach. I was confused, Master Montgomery. You remember how I get confused?'

Nestat did indeed remember. One particular incident of many came to mind, when MacGrip had somehow managed to fix a lead on a sucking pig and take it for a walk when he should have put it in the oven. Nipper the terrier never fully recovered from his ordeal.

'And I was grieving for your father,' he continued. 'I don't fully remember walking along the beach, but I must have. It was terri–'

'I know, I know,' Nestat consoled, 'but where did you go?'

'I was in a daze, but do remember people being particularly kind in Brighton, Weston-Super-Mare and Liverpool.'

'What!'

'I eventually arrived back at our beach again.'

'You mean to say you walked round the whole–?'

'I found the underside of the castle inhabited by a nasty piece of work. I lived in the stables and hid by day, eating the food kept in the old fall-out shelter.'

MacGrip lowered his voice. 'I heard terrible goings on, Master. Terrible they were. Then one day they were all gone. But yesterday someone returned and nearly caught me mowing the lawn. But fortunately I miscalculated and fell into the old well, and he missed me.'

'What did he want; do you have any idea?'

'No, but when I managed to climb out I did hear the sound of strange engines in the sky. Not a plane's engines, I hear those occasionally from the aerodrome over yonder. No, this was something big, and it was going slowly.'

'That's what it was,' said Nestat, bouncing the palm of his hand off his forehead.

'What's that?' said Hal.

'I'll tell you in a minute. We've got to get to the aerodrome.' He looked at MacGrip. 'I suppose the old jalopy isn't still in the stables?'

'I've serviced the late Master's car every year and charged the battery each week. Except for the six years I was away from Castle Montgomery.'

'Six years, you say. My, my. You mentioned you were armed when you came into the room?'

'Yes, sir, the gun is on the floor over there.'

'Nestat shone the light on an antique musket complete with bayonet.

'Maybe we'll leave that one for now. Right, MacGrip, let's get the old girl fired up, shall we?'

'Yes, sir!'

*

The three men dragged their feet though hundreds of clattering empty corned beef, baked bean and spam tins as they entered the run-down stables.

'This is what you've been living off, MacGrip?' said Nestat, shining the torch about.

'Yes, sir, although I did try and shoot some game in the woods at one time.'

'Did you have any luck?'

'I was certain I'd hit something because I heard a squeak. But I never found it. However, good fortune was on my side as I did come across an abandoned vehicle during my search. Someone had shot the driver in the neck. The milk, eggs and yoghurt were a welcome change. Of course, they played havoc with my intolerances.'

Nestat tutted but didn't inquire further. He knew the way and led on through a door into a large room. Instinctively, he flipped a light switch and, amazingly, a fluorescent tube flickered into life. There, sitting in the middle of a garage was a large object covered in a dust sheet.

Nestat smiled, walked over and removed the cover with a flourish, revealing a pristine Jensen Interceptor in royal blue.

'Only ten miles to the aerodrome, Hal, we'll be there in a jiffy.'

Hal pursed his lips and nodded approvingly. 'Nice wheels.'

'Father used the Jensen for trips to the golf club. Mother always used the Ferrari for shopping, as one does.'

'Sure, like one does,' said Hal.

'The keys are in the ignition, Master Montgomery,' said MacGrip.

Nestat and Hal climbed in.

Nestat grabbed the steering wheel and rolled his shoulders. 'See that - real walnut. They don't build them like this anymore.'

'No, they don't. It's a big old bus, though.'

'Yes, but with seven litres of V8 power it'll feel as nimble as a mini. Here we go.'

One turn of the key fired the engine into life.

'Listen to that,' said Nestat, giving it a few revs.

'Is it meant to shake like this?'

The engine had begun to misfire badly, with large bangs accompanying deep knocking sounds from the front. The car shook violently from side to side. A loud, terminal-sounding bang preceded a dent in the bonnet from the underside. Then silence.

'See how quietly she runs,' said MacGrip, not looking at them. 'I've kept her in tip-top condition.'

Nestat was about to say 'it's not running you old fool', but didn't. 'You've done a great job, MacGrip, but after spending hours in the cab getting here I think Hal and I could use some exercise. Out you get, Hal.'

'But the old git has—'

Nestat poked him in the ribs, shook his head and put a finger to his lips.

'Yeah, great job, MacGrip,' said Hal, rubbing his side as he climbed out of the car.

Nestat approached the old retainer, pointed him in the right direction and gave him a hug. 'I'll be in touch, old friend. Keep up the good work until I return.'

'You will come back, won't you, Master Montgomery?' The man was close to tears again.

'I promise. And thanks for everything. I'll get on the case about renovating the castle once I've concluded some important business in Iceland.'

'Iceland?' Hal mouthed.

'But until then, take care of yourself. The first chance I get I'll arrange for a regular delivery of food and other supplies from the village. Goodbye, MacGrip.'

They unlatched the garage door and left. Nestat turned to see the old man waving at the hay loft.

'Okay, Hal, time to burn some shoe leather.'

'You mean rubber.'

'In your case, yes.'

'What's this about Iceland?'

'I'll fill you in on the way. Now get running.'

SOMEWHERE NOT SO NICE AFTER ALL
THURSDAY MORNING, ICELAND

It took almost forty minutes for the airship to dock. Margot De Witte took full advantage of the delay and caught precious minutes of semi-sleep as every second counted; she had to be as alert as possible for what lay ahead.

'Would you like to come with me, Mrs De Witte,' said a voice.

She opened her eyes and saw a blue suit standing next to her. He differed from the airborne division by way of looking smart and well-pressed, with gold embroidered initials BVS on the top pocket of his jacket. He was also young and quite good looking.

'Have you managed to tie this balloon down at last?' she said, followed by a smile.

The young man returned her smile. 'I apologise for the delay – gusting wind.'

'I trust Doctor Slash isn't responsible?'

'I'm sorry?' His puzzled expression cracked and he laughed. 'Oh, I see. Slash – gusting wind – because he farts so much – that's funny.'

She stood and stretched. Patting the bag at her side she said, 'Let's meet your boss then, shall we?'

She'd spoken with brevity, but the prospect of meeting her father had switched on a fountain of excitement. There had been too much to think about on the journey, but not now. Outwardly calm, she reminded herself, outwardly calm.

As they walked, she asked the man, 'Where *is* Doctor Slash, I haven't seen him for a while?'

'He's waiting on the train.'

'Train?'

'We have a monorail from the airstrip, it'll take you into The Baron's headquarters.'

'Mm, I'm impressed.'

They reached the exit and there it was, a bright blue monorail train waiting at the end of a metal walkway.

They set off towards it, but after a few metres the young man slipped on something and almost fell. 'That damn monkey,' he said, stopping a moment to inspect the sole of his shoe before scraping it on the edge of the walkway. 'The thing goes everywhere with Slash – I mean The Doctor.'

'You don't have to be PC with me, young man. And you're correct, the monkey *does* go everywhere. Do you know why he keeps it?'

They started walking again. 'I've no idea, but The Baron has monkeys as well, something to do with an experiment. I don't understand; it's all very odd.'

'You seem like a nice young man, why are you working for a madman like Baron Von Sheit?'

'I'm doing a gap year at university and this job meets my degree criteria.'

'And what degree would that be?'

'People management and social welfare, I'm at Oxford, by the way. '

'At Oxford?' De Witte tried not to appear unduly disappointed. 'I studied at Oxford some years ago. It would appear times have changed.'

'You studied at Oxford Brooks?' he said with excitement.

'Oxford what?'

'Oxford Brooks. Obviously you've not heard of it. It's kind of newish.'

'I studied at the oldish one; that is unless they've knocked it down and built a car park.'

'You're funny.' He winked and said suggestively, 'Would you like to have a drink later, in my quarters?'

'I don't think that would be appropriate, do you?'

They ran out of walkway. Slash stumbled out of the train to greet her.

'It would appear the good doctor has come to my rescue. It's been interesting to meet you...?

'Gordini – Vincent Gordini. My father's Italian.'

'I would never have guessed,' she said with a look a mother would give a child that had just completed potty training. 'Good bye, Vincent.' She turned to meet Slash, leaving the young man to walk dejectedly back to the airship.

'Are you rested, Margot?' asked Slash.

The doors closed and the train set off.

'Reasonably, yes,' she said taking a seat. Spank sat opposite, eating a Snickers. 'Why do you keep feeding that poor creature ammunition, Doctor?'

'What – Oh I see what you mean?' He wheezed with laughter as he sat down next to Spank. 'He can't help it; there's something wrong with his digestive system.'

Spank threw him a look and resumed eating.

'I'm not surprised feeding him all that rubbish. And why do you have his mummified arm hanging round your neck; I assume it is his?'

Slash fixed his gaze on her bag. 'The reason is in there, Margot. But all in good time, you'll see why later today.'

De Witte shuddered and didn't enquire further.

Lights came on automatically as the train entered a

tunnel, and a few minutes later it slowed and stopped at an underground station.

Although she had never met him before, De Witte instantly recognised The Baron. He stood on the platform flanked by two well-dressed body guards and a bruiser of a man with an eye-patch. Unlike all The Baron's men she'd met so far, Mr Eye-Patch was dressed in black from head to toe. The doors opened and she walked out to meet her father's kidnapper.

The Baron stepped forward and stretched out his arm. 'Welcome to my humble home, Mrs De Witte.'

She declined the handshake. 'Where's my father?'

The arm fell to his side. 'Wilberforce told me you were blunt. May I address you as Margot?'

'If you must. The question remains.'

The Baron's eyes glanced nervously at Slash. 'He's, eh, on a day trip and will not be returning until this evening.'

'Why would he go on a trip if he knew I was arriving today?'

'We were not certain of your exact arrival time, Margot. Airships can be a little unpredictable in poor weather conditions.'

'All right, but you'll not see this,' she said, patting her bag, 'until I see him.'

He broke into a short mirthless laugh. 'He's not a prisoner, Margot. My men merely escort him for his convenience.'

'Of course they do,' she said sarcastically. 'It stays in my bag.'

'Very well, but I promise you *will* see him this evening. But enough of this banter. Hans!'

The man in black stepped forward.

'May I introduce Hans, my concierge,' said The Baron. 'He will escort you to your suite. I'm sure you would love to freshen up after the journey. Your suitcase should already be there.'

'No Father, no book.'

'Indeed,' said The Baron. 'We can wait. Time is our friend.'

She looked at Hans staring at her cleavage. 'Don't try anything funny, will you, Hans.'

He answered with a croak from the back of his throat.

'What's the matter – lost your tongue?'

'Yes, he has actually,' said The Baron. 'And some other bits as well.' He pointed towards Hans' groin area. 'So you are quite safe. I must have a chat with Wilberforce, please excuse me. I look forward to our meeting later. Good day, Margot.'

Hans gave something akin to a Nazi salute to The Baron and beckoned De Witte to follow him.

With a final glance at The Baron, Doctor Slash and the monkey, who was doing what he did best on the feet of one of the bodyguards, De Witte left the station platform for a tunnel.

*

The Baron held his smile until Margot De Witte was out of sight. He faced Slash, his forehead creased with worry. 'We've got a little problem. Walk with me to my office, Wilberforce.'

After going a short distance into a tunnel signposted "To the office", The Baron said sheepishly, 'I shot De Witte's father.'

Slash stopped. 'What! Why on earth did you do that?'

'It was an accident.'

'I've never known someone so accident-prone.' Scratching away a bit of his chin as he thought, he said, 'I suppose he's dead?'

'I'm afraid so. I put him in a cupboard at the back room of my office. What are we going to do?'

'Let me think,' said Slash.

They walked in silence with Spank scampering behind until they reached the office. Once inside, The Baron said, 'Have you had any ideas, Wilberforce?'

'Yes I have, actually.'

The Baron's face brightened. 'Wonderful! Does it involve shooting Margot De Witte? I mean, her father is dead and the poor thing will be distraught when she hears the news. I'll gladly oblige. It'll be a kindness.'

'My dear Hardinger, you really must stop shooting things – and no, it doesn't involve killing De Witte. She'll destroy the book at the first sign of trouble.'

'Then what are we going to do?' said The Baron, becoming agitated. 'What grand plan have you thought up?'

'Simple, we bring her father back to life. She'll have to give us the book to do that, otherwise he'll remain dead. It will be a bit tricky, and we'll need to get the timing right, but it will work.'

'And my darling wife?' said The Baron, touching a tear about to leave his eye.

Slash smiled. 'Here's the other good bit. Wouldn't it be wise to experiment with someone else before using the ritual on her – just in case we need to iron out a few technicalities?'

The Baron's expression changed in an instant to schoolboy delight. He clapped his hands together. 'Excellent! You are an accomplished evil genius, Wilberforce.'

Slash rubbed one of his claws on the front of his shell suit. 'So are you, Hardinger. Your volcano headquarters are the envy of the fraternity.'

'You'll soon have your own, as I promised. I'm going to put your name forward for the Devious Plan Medal.'

'You're too kind,' said Slash, his careless toss of the head rather spoilt by his hat and partial hairpiece falling off.

*

Had anyone been paying particular attention to Spank, at this moment in time, they might have caught a glimpse of him looking up at the trapdoor above the giant tank and they might reasonably have surmised that he was looking mournful, as if something dear that he had once lost was up there, somewhere. Then, it might have been noted by a keen observer that, for no readily identifiable reason, he began swapping the Post-it notes stuck above the array of coloured buttons on the Baron's desk. But nobody had been paying particular attention to Spank, at that moment in time.

IT'S ALL ABOUT WAGNER
THURSDAY MORNING, DAWN, ARGYLLSHIRE, SCOTLAND

'Brace up,' said Nestat, 'we're nearly there. The aerodrome is up ahead.'

'Oh, bugger this, I'm finished!' Hal stopped, his heavy breaths forming clouds in the cold air. He had only moments to recover before Nestat swept him up in a fireman lift and pressed onwards.

'Margot,' said Nestat, 'is bound for Iceland, as we are.'

The road had reached the crest of a heather-covered hill. In the distance the sun announced its intended arrival with a barely discernible pale glow behind the white-flecked sea, but it was an airdrome below with an airship mast that held Nestat's attention

'I was right. It's all fitting into place.' He rolled Hal's body onto the grass 'Are you alright?'

'I'm dying,' said Hal, clutching his belly and not making any attempt at movement.

'Don't be such a baby. Here, give me your hand.'

Nestat pulled him to his feet. 'That's it, take deep breaths. You'll be fine. Did you hear what I said?'

'Yeah, I did,' said Hal, bent double, but beginning to recover. 'Why Iceland?'

'The volcano, Eyjafjallajökull. I'm guessing Slash has his new headquarters there.'

'Eyjafjallajökull?'

'It was circled on the map. Then there was the model on the table at Witherspoon and Smythe?'

A dim light of realisation lit up Hal's eyes. 'Not Slash. Von Sheit.'

'Who?'

'Von Sheit.' Hal's breathing had returned to normal. 'Von Sheit's name was on that volcano model.'

A measure of Nestat's confidence drained away. 'Sheit was also on the map. Who is this Von Sheit?'

Hal straightened his body and arched his back. 'I hoped we were only dealing with Slash and De Witte. Baron Von Sheit is beyond evil.'

Nestat used his binoculars to scan the aerodrome for undesirables. 'Is he now? And what has he to do with Slash?'

'Oh,' said Hal, 'you don't see it, do you? It's the book.'

In his pursuit of revenge, Nestat had forgotten the book, forgotten *Liber Nigellus* and the apparition of Great Aunt Nelly. 'Yes, of course … the book … Why the book?'

'The Agency thinks the book is just some old collector's piece, a bit of bait to get The Baron; they have no idea. Von Sheit is a nutter for weird antiques and buys or has them stolen all over the world. He's a spider holding the threads of a thousand crimes, but no one has ever tracked him to his lair. But if he has the book and knows what it can do then we are in deep, deep sh– '

'The Agency,' interrupted Nestat, 'why didn't they tell me this? I have the highest security clearance – I have level Z.'

'It's complicated, Nestat.'

'Well, un-complicate it for me, there's a good chap.'

'For a start, after the letters come the numbers.'

'Numbers?'

'Level Z is followed by level 1, then 2 and so on.'

'What?'

'I have level 7 clearance.'

'What?'

'I have access to some stuff that would make your toes curl. Stuff about aliens. Stuff about JFK. Stuff about how aliens killed JFK.'

'And The Agency trusted you, above me, with this intelligence?'

'Yes.'

'What else do you know?'

'I know things about *Liber Nigellus* that even The Agency doesn't know.'

'Forget that damned book. Do you know anything about Slash? Is he working with this Baron?

'It's likely.'

'Right, then,' said Nestat, pointing to a hangar in the distance, 'there's a plane over there and it's taking us to Iceland.'

*

'Slash,' said Nestat, as they approached a run-down Portacabin close to the hangar, 'never struck me as the type to cosy up to anyone. I know he'll kill this Baron when he gets what he wants. It is in his nature.'

'But Margot is working with him ... isn't she? So why is she leaving all these breadcrumbs?' said Hal.

Nestat stopped and slapped his forehead. 'Of course, that's why Margot wants me to follow her. She is involved in some deal with Slash and she knows he'll kill her once he gets what he wants.'

They stopped outside the office. Music could he heard coming from within. Syncopated jazz.

Hal's brow creased. 'Wait,' he whispered.

'What?'

'I killed that man, didn't I?'

'Which man?'

'The one in Biggin Hill. I woke up covered in blood.'

'Why bring this up now?'

'Nestat,' said Hal, 'one time I woke up in the middle of a re-enactment of an ancient battle surrounded by unconscious men. I had a huge, blunted axe in my hands. Apparently I'd laid them all out. Quite a few had to go to hospital. I didn't even know I *was* a member of a re-enactment society.'

'We all forget things sometimes, Hal.'

'But that other side isn't me, Nestat; it's someone else. I have horrible dreams about hacking people up with a big sword. I'm eating more and more fish these days and have a hankering for reindeer meat. And I don't like Pringles anymore; I've always loved Pringles. I *am* possessed – you were right about that. I need the book to find out how to get rid of whatever it is inside me before I do something really bad. Before we go any further you need to know this.'

'Hal, you could have torn me limb from limb twice and you didn't. I think I'm safe.'

Hal nodded, but his expression indicated a troubled man.

Nestat gave him a friendly slap on the shoulder and turned his attention to fading words stencilled on a glass-panelled door of the Portacabin – *The Sid James Flying School.*

*

'Sid, it would be better for all concerned if you co-operated.'

An initial first glance around the messy flight office had told Nestat everything he needed to know about Sid's weaknesses, and strengths. A photograph of Sid in army uniform, holding a severed Iraqi head revealed he was no stranger to violence, so threats in this direction wouldn't wear. A picture of a wife and kid on the desk was a possibility. On second thoughts, she was frumpy and the kid didn't bare any resemblance to Sid. Then there was the Pirelli calendar on the wall with three love hearts circling the third of the month – an affair, perhaps? But it was a large photo on the wall showing Sid with a German shepherd, clearly taken recently, that hit the jackpot. Nestat decided to go through the motions, to find out if his appraisal had been correct.

Sid leaned back in his chair. 'No, I f-flippin' won't take you to Iceland. You can't make me f-fly. Shoot me you f-flippers. See if I care.'

Nestat pointed to Hal, who attempted a mean expression which at best suggested mild indigestion.

'And your big f-friend can f-flip off too.'

Nestat cleared space at the corner of the desk, and sat. 'I can appreciate your confidence, Sid. You're ex-forces. So am I. We can understand each other.'

'I'll understand you better when you give me f-five thousand quid.'

'I can give you a bit, Sid, but the rest will have to be on account.'

'Then the pair of you can f-flip off.'

Nestat picked up the picture of Sid's wife and child. 'What if I was to say we have a sniper trained on your wife as we speak? One phone call and–'

'You'd be doin' me a f-favour.'

Nestat fired a round into the calendar, obliterating the third of the month. Sid didn't flinch.

'What if I was to say we know about your little affair?'

'Little affair? I moved in with her last week. You don't know much.'

'We're Agency,' said Nestat, moving closer. 'We know everything.'

Sid's brow creased into a thousand lines. 'Agency? You're not part of that weird lot with the f-flippin' airship, are you? Or that limping cove who wanted the mast built? At least they coughed up plenty of dosh, not like you skin f-flints.'

Continuing to stare at Sid, Nestat lifted his arm and fired blind. The bullet hit the German shepherd's head, dead centre.

Sid slumped in his seat, his face resting in his hands. He looked up with a tear in his bloodshot eyes. 'You've got Wagner?'

He'd been right. The bluff was on. 'We studied you, Sid. You don't love your wife. That kid isn't yours. Your bit of fluff is just that – a bit of fluff. But Wagner? You love Wagner. And we don't want to hurt him.'

'Sid began to sob. 'You're as bad as that f-flippin' woman.'

'Woman?' Nestat eased off the desk.

'Yeah, said if I didn't give her the key to the gent's toilet she'd make sure Wagner got a poisoned Boneo. What she wanna use the gents' toilet for anyway? Just one of them perverts, like the lot with her, all wearing stupid blue suits. Bunch of poofs.'

He began to sob again, opened a drawer and fumbled inside. 'Where's that bottle of whisky – and why's everyone got it in for Wagner?

'I need a leak, Hal. Keep an eye on him. Give me the key, Sid.'

*

'Now, what am I looking for?' said Nestat, taking in the grubby details of the small toilet: a blocked urinal, broken mirror with no writing on it – too obvious anyway. He pulled out what was left on a towel dispenser and felt inside – nothing. Slowly pushing the door open to the lavatory, he gagged and kicked the lid down with his foot. Turning to leave, he noticed some debris on the floor, barely discernible amongst faded Razzle magazines and screwed up tissues. Looking up he saw a small hole in the plasterboard ceiling. Balancing on the toilet, he stretched up and felt inside.

A broad smile broke across his face. 'Chin, chin, Margot. I'm on my way.'.

PLOT HOLE
THURSDAY LUNCHTIME, CANARY WHARF, LONDON

Sven closed the heavy door of the large, impressive office and looked at the man sitting behind the mahogany desk in front of floor-to-ceiling tinted glass. In his late fifties, he looked well-preserved and fit, slightly tanned with good skin and a full head of wavy, brown hair. He'd expected some old buffer, not a dapper man about town, and knight of the realm to boot.

'I guess you're Sir Hector Chisholm,' he said as he stopped in front of the desk.

Sir Hector peered over the top of rimless glasses with a disdainful expression. 'And you are?'

'Max Farlow, Private Detective.'

Sir Hector leaned forward and pressed a button on the intercom. 'My secretary informed me you were from Isotope Commodities. Good day, Mr Farlow.'

A voice on the intercom said, 'Yes, Sir Hector.'

'Monica, can you–'

Sven coolly pressed his finger on the red button, killing the call.

'What do you think you're doing?'

Sven curled his lip. 'Let's keep this personal, I'm not

113

into threesomes.'

'I beg your pardon?'

'Let's just say I've got the goods and they're for your ears only.'

'What on earth are you on about, man?'

The woman came back on the intercom. 'Is everything alright, Sir Hector?'

Sven narrowed his eyes. 'Trust me, pops, if you don't listen to what I'm going to say you'll regret it, big time.'

Sir Hector's finger hovered over the intercom. Sven read the indecision and nailed it with, 'Not tonight Josephine.'

He went pale and pressed the button. 'Yes, everything is fine, Monica. I'll call if I need you.' He sat back in his chair, surveying Sven with calculating eyes. 'How do you know about this?'

'Sleaze is my backyard, pops. But let's just say a little bird told me.'

'Can you speak to me in English, please? I want to know how you found out.'

Sven pointed to a chair facing the desk.

Sir Hector nodded.

He sat down, leant back, almost went over backwards, recovered, and crossed his legs. 'A client secured my services to find their runaway daughter. After a lot of checking and shoe leather I found her living in Queensway, working as a hooker.'

Sir Hector went a shade paler.

'I said her family was looking for her; she said she didn't want to be found. She also said they'd kill her if they knew what she was doing.'

'Are they religious fanatics?'

Sven shook his head, sucked air through his teeth and said, 'Sicilian, with Mafia connections.'

Sir Hector's eyes widened.

Sven enjoyed the effect. Cheesewright the truck driver no longer existed.

'Go on,' Sir Hector croaked.

'Well ...' Sven, took a second to nonchalantly pick a tooth with his fingernail and inspect the end. '... This is where it gets interesting. I told her I wanted my fee for finding her, she said there was a lot more to be had if I kept my mouth shut. That's when she told me about you, Wellington.'

'She didn't know my name.'

'So I heard. But you should be more careful where you leave your jacket in future.'

'She went through my pockets?'

'Cruel old world, innit, pops?'

Sir Hector's expression soured. 'So this is blackmail – you want money.'

'Yep, I want holdin' foldin', and plenty of it.'

With a baffled expression, he shook his head.

'Moolah, spondulaks, dosh.' Sven sighed. 'Money.'

'Why should I pay you off, Mr Farlow? In the light of what you've just told me she isn't about to make her story public. It would be your word against mine.'

Sven went over the various scenarios Tommy had drummed into his head and dealt a killer punch. 'You're wrong, pops. If you don't play ball she'll flower up the tale, call in a few friends to back it up – you know: *good Sicilian Catholic girl forced into sex slavery*', that kind of thing. She'd have nothing to lose. I get my fee, her brothers cart her off to Palermo, she'd be forgiven and marry some rich wop and you'd be on a hit list. Then again, given the choice she'd prefer to go it alone. Get my drift?'

Sir Hector gulped.

'But I can think of a million reasons to buy our silence.'

'A million pounds!'

Sven grinned. 'She'll vanish to the other side of the planet, I'd suffer permanent amnesia and Lady Chisholm and the tabloids need never know.'

Sir Hector removed his glasses, ran his hands through his hair and stared at the desk.

Sven could hardly contain his excitement as he watched him wrestle with his thoughts. Wishing Tommy were here to see it, he waited for close to half a minute, relishing the position of advantage, before saying, 'Well, what's it to be, pops?'

Sir Hector fixed his eyes on him, his haggard face transforming into a shrewd expression. 'Who else knows about this?'

'Just you, me and the girl – our little secret.'

Sir Hector leant back in the chair, and if Sven had been the observant type he would have picked up the glint in his eyes and a change in body language. 'To use your lingua franca, you have set me up, Mr, Farlow, if that is your real name.'

'Now hold on a minute–'

Sir Hector cut him dead. 'I'm not taken in by all this Marlowe-esque tomfoolery. I recognise an act when I see one – and a not very convincing one at that. However, you and the girl could cause considerable trouble for me so I shall acquiesce to your threat of blackmail on certain conditions: the girl must be present when I hand over the money; I want to make it clear what will happen to both of you should you renege on our deal. You see, Mr Farlow, blackmailers have a nasty habit of coming back for more. This will never happen. I will have recorded proof you have blackmailed me, and if worse comes to worst I'll make the recording available to the police. You'll both go to prison. Do you understand me?'

Sven didn't react, but Sir Hector appeared satisfied by what he saw. He continued, 'Therefore, I pick the location where the handover is to be made. And it is to be fifty thousand, not a million.'

Sven squirmed in the chair. This was going dreadfully wrong. He racked his brain for an answer but the script didn't have one, leaving him to wing it with a last ditch one-liner. 'I'm calling the shots here, pops, not you.'

Sir Hector leant forward over the desk; Sven recoiled at

his venomous expression.

'Not any more. If that whore is the daughter of a Sicilian family then I'm the man on the moon. That is the deal, take it or leave it.'

Sven suddenly felt very hot in the raincoat. 'I'll have to contact her and get—'

He cut him short again by wagging a finger. 'You'll call her now and tell her to meet you at the Hanleigh Hotel in Knightsbridge this evening, at nine. Tell her I have a private suite. You will be staying here with me.'

Sven opened his mouth but no words came out.

'I'm waiting,' said Sir Hector, drumming his fingers on the desk.

Sven took the mobile out of his pocket. Covering the keypad with one hand he made the call with the other, careful not to use any names. Vicky appeared calm on hearing the news. She reassured him, told him to do what he was told and hung up. Sven fumbled the buttons and deleted the call registry.

Sir Hector nodded. 'Very good. Now give me the phone, without the SIM card if you wish.'

Sven complied. He only had Vicky's words of reassurance to stop him running out of the building and not stopping until he reached Dover.

'Excellent,' said Sir Hector. 'Make yourself comfortable in reception. I'll tell Monica to keep you fed and watered whilst I arrange for the money to be made available. Do not leave the building, otherwise our deal is off. I will alert security, just in case it slips your mind. Goodbye for now, Mr Farlow. Or whatever your name is.'

Sven walked out of the office with a great deal less swagger than when he had entered, and it was Cheesewright the truck driver who sat wobbly-kneed in reception reading a magazine article about Sir Hector Chisholm being presented with a black belt in karate.

*

Sir Hector smiled as the office door closed. He rose from

the chair, walked over to a drinks cabinet, poured a stiff whisky and downed it in one. Back at his desk, he picked up the phone.

'Security – I have a guest coming to meet you. Mr Farlow. Make him comfortable, but frisk him thoroughly, in case he's carrying a wire. And make sure he doesn't wander off.'

He put the phone down and opened the top left drawer in his desk, removing a small black, leather-bound book. He flicked through a few pages and stopped at one on which a business card had been stuck: *Professional Cleaning Services.*

'I'll be out of pocket, Mr Farlow, but you and your little prostitute will not be getting a penny.'

FLURDEBURDEKULL AND THE INVISIBLE VOLCANO

THURSDAY MORNING, SCOTLAND

'Have you been drinking, Sid?' said Nestat.

Sid wasn't so much seated at the controls of the Junkers 88, as slumped. 'Jusht checkin' the dialsh.'

The Second World War German bomber had been botched-up to carry a few passengers, but the large elongated bomb doors beneath Nestat and Hal's feet appeared well oiled and fully functional.

'There're no seat belts on these deck chairs, Sid,' said Hal.

A deep, raucous laugh met his observation.

'The in-flight service isn't up to much, either,' said Nestat, with a wink.

'I get airsick and don't like flying at the best of times.'

'Really, you surprise me?'

Hal huffed. 'Sid, when did this plane last receive its airworthiness certificate?'

Another raucous laugh. 'Right, we're taking off in a minute sho put y' parachutes on.'

'I want to get off,' said Hal.

'He's playing with you.'

'They're under your seats – hic.'

'Maybe not,' said Nestat, reaching under Hal's chair. 'Stand up. I'll help you.'

Hal stood rigid as Nestat strapped the parachute on. He had to ease the big man back into the chair, where he sat with his rucksack on his knees like a pile of lost luggage.

'Feel safer now?' said Nestat, giving him an encouraging pat on the head.

The frightened look suggested a negative.

No sooner had Nestat put on his own parachute and resumed his seat when a few bangs and puffs of black smoke heralded the powerful radial engines leaving idle speed. The plane slowly moved forward, vibrating, flexing and creaking.

Hal closed his eyes.

Nestat caressed the Rolex Oyster Perpetual.

The engines reached a new level of noise as full power sent them bouncing over the grass airstrip. After what seemed an interminable length of time the bouncing stopped, leaving only vibration and noise.

'How long, Sid?' Nestat shouted.

'What bit of Iceland did ye say you wanted again?'

'Close to that volcano that blew its top a few years back.'

'Three hours or there'bouts.'

Nestat reached down and picked up two foil parcels off the floor. He turned to Hal. 'Self-service. Sid made a few sandwiches, fancy one?'

Hal shook his head.

Nestat opened the foil. 'Mm, chopped pork and piccalilli.'

Hal vomited.

'You sure you won't have one?'

He gave an encore.

'On second thoughts, I think I'll eat them later. I'm going to catch a nap so give me a nudge after a bit, will you?'

Nestat dozed off, imagining sitting in a deck chair watching a cricket match on the village green: the sound of wood on willow; the clink of ice in a gin and tonic; the smell of grass after a warm summer shower. He knew how to switch off.

*

He woke to Hal's face almost touching his. Hal hadn't said anything, but a strong smell, that wasn't orange blossom, had cut short his intimate encounter with Lady Cynthia Biscuit in the orangery at Bourbon Hall.

'Are we there?'

'I won't do it!' said Hal.

'Won't do what?' said Nestat, coming fully awake and sitting up. 'Sid, what's going on?'

'You're jumping, that's what's going on!'

Sid had sobered up.

Nestat left his seat and went to the cockpit. 'Is the plane giving out?'

'Nope. I had a run in with air traffic control once.'

Nestat looked out of the window. 'Is that why we're flying fifty feet above the sea?'

'Yeah. Why should I have given way to a f-flippin' 747, eh? Sail over steam. I told 'em. Anyway, they'll arrest me if I land. I'm not getting locked up in a f-flippin' igloo for you f-flippers.'

Nestat placed a hand on the Walther. 'You said you would take us to Iceland.'

'Yeah, and I have, haven't I? I never said nuffin about landing. Why do y' think I told you to put on the parachutes?'

Nestat slid the gun out of its holster. 'Listen to me, Sid—'

'Can you f-fly a Junkers 88?'

He thought a moment. 'Good point. Look, I'll jump if I have to.' Lowering his voice, he nodded in the direction of Hal. 'But I'll never get him to do it.'

'Then he's going back to Scotland.'

Nestat glanced at Hal sitting white-knuckled in the deck-chair. He was a big guy and the thought of him having one of his funny turns wasn't a pleasant prospect. There was only one thing for it. He gave instructions to Sid and returned to his seat.

'You can relax, Hal, we're not going out the door.'

Hal's head spun sideways. 'We're not? Oh, thanks Nestat. I'd never be able to jump out of a plane.'

'I know, I know. We'll do a steep climb in a minute, circle the volcano then Sid will find a place to land.'

'Thank Odin this is nearly over. I began to feel a bit strange a second ago.'

Nestat breathed a sigh of relief; his idea hadn't come a moment too soon.

Five minutes passed and the plane began a steep climb, banking to the left. Hal kept his eyes closed, Nestat kept his on Sid.

After a few minutes Sid turned and gave a thumbs-up.

Nestat nodded, reached over to Hal and gripped the release cord on his parachute.

The bomb doors opened, and still in their deck-chairs, Nestat and Hal fell into the chill Icelandic sky.

*

Nestat landed on his feet. Hal didn't. He had remained in the deck-chair, which fell to earth with an almighty crash. Keeping his distance, Nestat watched for any signs of *Halgoth the Viking*. The big man emerged from under his parachute, turned to look at him, and grinned.

'Are you okay, Hal?'

'That was fantastic!' he said, standing and unbuckling the parachute.

'What?'

'Like floating.'

'You mean you enjoyed it?'

'Once I stopped screaming, yeah. You tricked me, though.'

'I had no choice.'

'I forgive you. Where are we?'

Nestat gave the terrain a three-sixty: desolate, ashy, rocky and not a tree in sight. 'That must be the volcano.' He pointed to a column of smoke rising from an ice covered mountain.

'Hold on,' said Hal, rummaging in his rucksack. 'GPS time.'

'Well done. Any sign of life nearby?'

After a bit of tapping, he said, 'There's a small village to the south, Flurdeburdekull, about four kilometres.'

'Good. We'll head there. Seems as good a place to start as any. We might be able to get some inside knowledge from the locals.'

'Nestat, I haven't got my passport with me.'

'And I haven't got any Icelandic Króna. But I think they're the least of our problems, don't you?'

Nestat considered the four passports, matching credit cards and US dollars hidden in the lining of his jacket. Perhaps a little tinkering could secure Hal a passage home? He gave the volcano a last glance and joined his partner walking down the barren hillside.

*

'This is good,' said Hal, tucking in to a large fish complete with head, smothered with gherkins and sour cream.

Nestat picked at green *things* floating in a bowl of clear broth. 'Seems like the US dollar still carries some clout,' he said, wondering what the green actually was as he subjected it to close scrutiny on the end of a spoon.

Hal wiped his mouth roughly on his sleeve. 'If this all pans out, I'm going to think about a holiday home here.'

'Really,' said Nestat, dropping the spoon in the bowl and pushing it away. 'You'd like to spend your hols in a village where there's one restaurant, two funeral parlours, six pharmacies and a retail outlet for army surplus breathing apparatus?'

Hal stopped chewing and gave the question some

thought. He nodded, resumed eating and said, 'Feels like home – the land of sagas and eddas. And they build good dragon ships.'

'What?'

'I mean, houses.'

'Hal, they're all made from asbestos and have oxygen tanks on the roofs. And the villagers – I've never seen such an unhealthy bunch in my life. Mind you, their English is good, I'll give them that.'

The gaunt, pasty-faced restaurateur had sidled up to the table, holding a terracotta tureen. 'Do you want more eating?'

Nestat had a quick look at the contents and declined. 'Tell me, does the volcano give you many problems?'

'What volcano is this?'

The man kept his eyes fixed on Hal, who was tucking in to his food with increasing gusto.

'What volcano? You can't be serious.'

'It's very hilly round here,' said the man not taking his eyes off Hal.

'Hilly? I'm talking about that big smoking lump of rock towering over your village that brought most of Europe's air traffic to a standstill.'

'I don't know what you're talking about,' said the man. 'You must have seen someone having a barbecue.'

'What?'

'Your friend is an interesting man.'

Nestat looked at Hal, whose dripping beard had now collected a considerable amount of fish bits. The big man paused, burped loudly and carried on chomping.

'I can think of a better word than interesting. Look, I need some information about–'

'Enjoy your meal.'

The man turned and left in a hurry, leaving a trail of slops on the floor from the tureen.

Nestat scratched the side of his head. 'Strange. Did you hear that, Hal?'

'Hear what? I want a horn of ale.'

'Say again?'

'Harold Bushy Feet has too much power. No one can prosper under his iron rule. I must kill him.'

'Hal?'

'Bring me drink!' He banged his fist on the table.

Nestat ground the chair back and stood, his hand already loosening the clip on the holster; it remained inside the jacket, hovering.

Halgoth the warlord glared at him with mad eyes.

Nestat tried to work out why Hal had changed. He wasn't scared or in pain, quite the reverse, he appeared to be enjoying himself. It had to be the fish or gherkins. No, he'd eaten those before and hadn't changed. The sour cream – that was it. Nestat reached over the table and grabbed the pot.

Hal moved quickly and his big hand began to squeeze his wrist with incredible strength.

'Leave it, or I'll tear your arm off,' growled Hal.

Nestat took the advice, rubbed his arm and stepped back a few paces. Engrossed with the problem in hand, he took little notice of shuffling feet from behind until hands grabbed his arms – lots of hands.

'What the hell's going on?' he said, struggling to break free.'

'Hold him tight.'

It was the voice of the restaurant owner, who walked past from behind and bowed before Hal. 'Halgoth, Warlord of the Beordeed and Master of the Haegarand, the saga foretold your return. Thank Odin, Thor and all the gods.'

The man held an aged, open book. He dropped on one knee and presented it to Hal. Nestat's eyes went from a drawing of a face in the book to Hal then back to the face again. They were nigh identical. A university gap-year spent at Reykjavik University studying ancient Icelandic and Nordic literature gave Nestat some background, but this was over and above the Icelander's obsession with their ancient past; this was very weird.

'Hal,' said Nestat, 'tell these men to unhand me.'

Halgoth looked him up and down. 'Why? You do not appear to be a warrior. Are you a necromancer? Do you have magic?'

A crowd closed in around Nestat, murmuring, 'Witchcraft, burn him.'

Halgoth gave him a penetrating look, shrugged his shoulders, picked up his knife and spoon and resumed eating. Between mouthfuls he said, 'Go on then, burn him.'

Nestat found himself being dragged backwards. 'Hal, it's me Nestat. What are you doing? We're here to kill–' He was about to say Slash, but checked himself. A stab in the dark was better than a bonfire in the street. 'We're here to kill Harold Bushy Feet, remember?'

Halgoth stopped eating.

The crowd continued to manhandle him towards the door of the restaurant, but using the Maltese wriggle method, taught to him by an ancient crowd-control expert in Valetta, he broke free and stepped back to face the villagers. He whipped out the gun, shot in the air then pointed it at Hal. 'If you make one move I'll blow the Viking's brains out!'

The villagers eyed him warily, but remained still.

Halgoth looked up at the hole in the ceiling. 'You have powerful magic. You say you wish to assist me in my quest?'

Nestat thought quickly. 'I can use my magic to help you kill Harold.'

'It's not magic, it's a gun,' said someone from the crowd. 'I want to see him burn.'

Halgoth pointed to the person who had spoken out. 'Use your magic on him. If it works then I will take you as my councillor.'

Nestat turned to see the villagers drifting away from a

youth with a spotty complexion and weasel eyes until he stood alone, trembling.

Nestat had drawn a line at shooting innocent people, children, racing pigeons and kelp, but needs must. He aimed carefully and pulled the trigger.

The young man howled in pain and jumped about on one foot.

Halgoth roared with laughter. 'I like this. Do it to the other foot.'

Nestat faced Hal. 'I don't want to use all my magic on this ignorant Skræling when it can best serve our purposes against Harold.'

Hal's eyes narrowed, and for a moment Nestat feared the worse, but he nodded and said, 'You are also wise, Nestatling. I will seek your council before we attack. But enough of this jesting and feasting. Where is my sword?'

As the wounded young man was escorted from the restaurant so an elderly one was led in, bearing something long wrapped in hessian cloth. He stopped before Hal, creaked onto one knee and held out the bundle. Hal took it, shook off the cloth and drew a long sword from its scabbard. He swung the blade with a series of rapid cuts and thrusts then held it aloft.

The villagers fell to their knees shouting, 'All hail Halgoth and his mighty sword, *Leg Cobbler*.'

Nestat thought it wise to follow suit, and shuffled on his knees to the restaurant owner. 'Psst, whatever your name is, where does Harold Bushy Feet live?'

'My name is Lars and the tyrant lives inside the volcano. All hail Halgoth and his mighty sword, *Leg Cobbler*.'

'You told me there was no volcano.'

'You could have been from the European aviation board. All hail...'

Nestat said, 'So you do have at least one of your feet planted in the twenty-first century.'

Lars stopped chanting and faced Nestat. 'You think us

a backward people full of superstition, but you are wrong. We are a nation of authors and are well-educated. Our sagas are the foundation blocks of European literature.'

'Oh, I know. It's just,' Nestat flicked his head towards Hal, 'this bit.'

'You are foolish, Nestatling. How do you expect us to fight dragons and trolls without Halgoth, Warlord of the Beordeed and Master of the Haegarand?'

'Of course, forgive me. My knowledge of mythical beasts is a bit rusty.'.

THE KNIGHTS OF KNIGHTSBRIDGE
THURSDAY EVENING, LONDON

Tommy took a moment to appreciate Penny, who was oblivious to his close proximity. The last time he'd seen her was rushed and desperate. Now, calm, collected and with the vividness of sobriety, it struck him just how beautiful she was. In a dark cashmere coat with her equally dark hair gathered into the collar, she looked about in search of him, her one time fiancé, Tommy Boyle. He could see her breath clearly: sweet breath passing over lips he had kissed so many times. Those lips had only brushed his cheek since Hector had come on the scene. The days of love, laughter and passion were gone. He wanted them back. He wanted his name back.

The traffic lights changed and the cab lurched forward, stopping outside South Kensington tube station. Tommy opened the door and called out to her. With a stern expression she walked over and climbed in, bringing with her a waft of perfume and cold air. The cab set off.

Tommy broke an awkward silence. 'Thanks for coming, Penny.'

'I've left a note for Hector, so if I'm not back before he comes home from his club then he'll come looking for me

– with the police.'

'Oh come on, Penny?' He felt her mistrust deeply. 'I'm not here to trick you but to let you hear the truth – maybe to give me another chance.'

'I hope that's the case – to hear the truth, that is'

'You'll know in,' Tommy checked his watch, 'less than forty minutes.'

'And all this cloak and dagger stuff is necessary?'

'Look, Penny, I'm sober and in my right mind. You are going to hear it from the horse's mouth, so to speak. Please trust me like you used to, just this once?'

She bit her lip, turned away from him and stared out the window. 'This one last time, Tommy,' she said quietly.

'Thanks. But you must do exactly what I tell you when we get to the hotel.'

She turned quickly to face him with a look of alarm. 'You're taking me to a hotel?'

'Don't worry, it's not like that,' he reassured her. 'This meeting is taking place in a hotel. You'll be listening on an ear piece – this one.' He reached in his pocket and gave her a small earphone. 'All you have to do is hear a conversation, nothing more.'

'And this will prove you're innocent?'

'Yes, I hope so. But you must promise me you'll wait until everything is over. Whatever happens, don't try to find me; it's very important. The people involved must never know you're listening. Do you promise?'

She nodded. 'And what happens afterwards?'

'You'll know the reason why I went off the rails. Then it'll be up to you to decide what to do. I won't interfere, your call, and whatever it is I'll go along with it.'

'Okay, for old time's sake. But this is a bit scary – like a spy movie.'

Tommy took a deep breath and exhaled loudly. 'I've got butterflies myself. I wish I didn't have to do this, but enough is enough.' He touched her black, woollen gloved hand resting on the seat. 'Thanks again, Penny.'

She smiled weakly and didn't pull her hand away.

He took this as a good sign.

*

They followed the waiter to a table in the hotel restaurant, one Tommy had checked out earlier during a frenzied afternoon of preparation. Through a small gap in a wood and glass partition he could indirectly see the entrance lobby and front door. The waiter gave them the menus and left.

'You choose, Penny,' he said, checking his watch.

'Don't you want to look at the menu?'

'I'm not hungry. Pick anything you like for me.' He kept his eyes fixed on the foyer.

'Do you want a bottle of wine?'

'Eh? No thanks.'

'You *have* changed, Tommy. When do I put the ear thingy in?'

'Not yet. I'll tell you when.'

She began to speak again but he didn't hear her. Sir Hector Chisholm had entered the hotel, followed by a gaunt and dejected Sven Cheesewright and two hard-looking men with crew cuts. They turned the corner towards the lift, disappearing from his line of sight.

'So it's smoked salmon with capers, followed by steak tartare.'

'Mm,' Tommy looked at her for a brief second. 'Yeah, that'll be great.' He turned his attention to the door again, just in time to see Vicky come in, looking wonderful.

'I have to go to the loo, Penny'

'Shall I put in the—'

'Not yet. Wait till I get back. I won't be long.'

He went into a cubicle in the toilet and fitted an ear piece. If the technology worked then he should be able to hear what was going on in Vicky's life at that very moment. He heard a high-pitched whine, followed by a low buzzing sound and then entered Vicky's world. He heard lift doors open, silence for some seconds then a rap on a door.

*

'It sounds like your lady friend has arrived, Mr Farlow,' said Sir Hector. 'Be a gent and let her in, will you.'

Sven dragged his feet over the carpet and opened the door of the suite. Vicky stepped in, smiled at everyone and pushed the door almost closed behind her.

'Who the hell are *you*?' said Sir Hector.

'A work colleague of Napoleon,' said Vicky, sweetly.

'What!' He turned on Sven. 'You said you and the girl were the only ones.'

Sven opened his mouth and did an impression of a fish out of water.

Vicky gave Sven a look which said, "Keep your mouth shut," and replied for him, 'He told you the truth – then. But my friend was worried and let me in on her secret.'

Sir Hector breathed deeply and stared at the floor. The goons walked over and stood next to him. Finally, he looked up with a murderous expression. 'You or Detective Moron here will tell me where she is or the deal is off.'

Vicky kept her back to the door and said matter-of-factly, 'I don't think so. You used and degraded my friend and you're going to pay for it.'

'Degraded?' He fumed. 'She's a whore. I didn't hear her complain when I paid her.'

Vicky smiled.

Sir Hector's eyes lit up. 'Hold on a moment.' He turned to one of the goons. 'Search her. She's recording this.'

'Touch me and I'll scream the house down,' said Vicky.

'Do what you've been paid for,' said Sir Hector.

Simultaneously the men reached inside their jackets and produced guns. Sven buckled at the knees and held on to a side table to prevent him falling.

Vicky said weakly, 'You'd shoot us, murder us?'

'If you don't do as you're told. Now come here and be searched.'

Vicky complied.

The goon searched her, then her bag. He pulled out a mobile. 'She's got it on record,' he said with a grin, handing the phone to Sir Hector.

'Dear me, how very amateurish – do you take me for a fool? I'm not going to be caught out with that one, particularly by idiots like you. Now tell me what I want to know.'

The two men levelled their guns, one at Vicky's head and the other at Sven's.

*

Tommy rushed back to the table in the restaurant.

'You took your time,' said Penny. 'I've ordered.'

'I've got to go again, Penny. Count off a couple of minutes then put the earphone in. This is it. Have you got that, a couple of minutes then put it in – and remember what I said earlier, don't budge an inch until I get back. Okay?'

'Yes, alright, but–'

Tommy was already in the foyer and heading for the stairs.

*

Vicky had barely begun to spin her yarn to Sir Hector when the Viscotti brothers barged through the unlatched door, their guns drawn and instantly levelled at Sir Hector.

'Don't do anything crazy,' said Michael Viscotti, directing his words at the goons. 'Unless you wanna see his brains on the carpet.'

The goons shifted their aim to the brothers, but the guns noticeably wobbled in their hands. 'D-Drop your g-guns,' said one, his words trailing to a silent whimper.

'I don't think so,' said Vincenzo Viscotti with a grin. 'Oh, I get it. You think this is a Mexican standoff. But I've got two guns.' He pulled another automatic from his shoulder holster. 'You still wanna play?'

'Now, you boys skedaddle,' said Michael Viscotti, his facial tick and sideways smile the very embodiment of psychopathy.

Vincenzo flicked off the safety catches with his thumbs. 'And we'll forget your faces. But don't go getting no police or we'll be calling; we know where you come from. Our business is with this thing.' He pointed one gun at Sir Hector. 'He messed with our sister.'

Sir Hector, who had remained transfixed throughout, said, 'Your sister really is Sicilian?'

'You bet your arse she is,' said Vincenzo.

The two goons exchanged fearful glances but didn't move. One said, 'You g-gonna k-kill him?'

'Maybe, maybe not,' said Michael with an icy stare. 'But unless you two piss off now we're gonna do you all.'

Both men looked at each other, nodded, muttered apologies to Sir Hector and walked to the door, sheepishly pocketing their guns on the way.

Sir Hector shouted after them, 'You lousy cowards!'

One turned before leaving. 'You're in a different league, mister. Call someone else next time.'

The door closed. Sir Hector looked at Vicky, his nostrils flared. 'You lying bitch! You told your thugs everything.'

Vicky smiled sardonically. 'Insurance. I guessed you'd play dirty. Mr. Farlow did warn you what would happen if you did.'

Vincenzo fixed his gaze on Sir Hector. 'You force my sister to have the sex with you?'

'I didn't force her. She agreed and I paid her.'

'So, you saying my sister is a whore?' said Michael, his eyes narrowing.

'Yes. I mean no. What are you doing?'

Vincenzo holstered his guns and took out a stiletto knife. With a flick of the wrist, the blade shot out. 'I'm gonna cut you up a treat, that's what.' He stepped forward.

Sir Hector wrung his hands together. 'This can't be happening. I didn't know she was your sister. I thought she was a... Please don't.'

WHAT, A SAGA?
THURSDAY EVENING, ICELAND

'This is up to date, Lars?' said Nestat.

'Yes, it was taken two weeks ago. We managed to salvage the camera from the wreckage.'

Nestat looked up from the A2-sized aerial photograph of the volcano and raised an eyebrow in question.

'The balloon was attacked by a dragon,' said Lars

'You saw this?'

'Yes, a trail of fire and smoke.'

'And did this *dragon* appear long, thin-ish with stubby wings and a pointy nose?'

Lars nodded.

'Ah, right, a surface-to-air dragon. You said an airship arrived this morning.' Nestat pointed to an area on the volcano. 'It went here?'

'Yes.'

Nestat nodded. 'There's a monorail leading from what looks like a docking area. It vanishes into the side of the mountain. Is this the only way in?'

'No, above the village is the main entrance. Wait one minute, Nestatling.' Lars left the kitchen-cum-HQ.

Nestat drummed his fingers on the table. Trays of fish

surrounded him in different stages of dying, drying, pickling, steaming, poaching and a process he'd never seen before which unsettled his stomach. He wanted to joke with Hal that Witherspoon and Smythe would have felt at home here, but the big man, slumped in a chair in the corner and snoring loudly, didn't look like Hal anymore, just a drunken Viking after ten horns of ale.

Lars reappeared, followed by a young, blond-haired man wearing a bloodied sling and supporting himself with a wooden crutch.

'Flonogson is the postman,' said Lars. 'He will help you.'

'*Was* the postman,' said Flonogson, throwing a venomous glance at Lars.

'You look the worse for wear,' said Nestat.

'That old git in the volcano shot me. I'm lucky to be alive.'

'You were given no warning it was dangerous?' said Nestat.

'Nope. Nice of them not to tell me wasn't it? I'm a hero now. My name will be in a saga. Well they can stuff that. "Postman required: good salary, free accommodation and fringe benefits." I only found out what the fringe benefits were when they dug the bullets out in the clinic.'

Nestat looked at him quizzically.

'A ruddy funeral plan, that's what. I'm going back to Reykjavik as soon as I can walk properly.'

Nestat turned to Lars, who shrugged. 'He didn't read the small print.'

'Look, this is getting nowhere,' said Nestat. 'I sympathise, Flonogson, really I do, but can you give some information that will help me get into Baron Von—'

'Hem, hem,' Lars interrupted.

Nestat rolled his eyes. 'Harold Bushy Feet's fortress?'

'I'll tell *you* what I can. As for this lot here,' Flonogson threw another sideways glance at Lars, 'The Baron can use them for target practice for all I care.'

Lars didn't comment this time.

'Tell me what you know, please?' said Nestat.

'Well, I walked up to the front door and rang the bell. I had a package and needed a signature.'

'There's a front door; no machine gun nests, missiles, henchmen?'

'Nope, just an ordinary front door in a cliff, weird or what? It's a bit scorched, though.'

'Right, so you rang the bell, and?'

'This tubby guy with a monocle answered. He smiled, signed my form and asked me if I had a wife or sweetheart. I told him no, so he pulls out a gun shoots me in the leg. As I hopped off he got me in the arm as well.'

'Just like that?'

'Yep. The bullets were pinging off rocks all around me.'

Nestat turned to Lars and shook his head in disbelief.

'We were waiting for Lord Halgoth,' said Lars defensively. 'Flonogson is the twelfth messenger. The saga read, when eleven have died and the twelfth nearly dies then Halgoth would return and defeat the tyrant in his fortress.'

'The cemetery's full of ruddy postmen,' said Flonogson. 'They're all flipping bonkers.'

'I'm inclined to agree with him,' said Nestat.

'Listen,' said Lars. 'If the fortress hadn't been built then the tyrant wouldn't have come here. And if he hadn't then Halgoth, Warlord of the Beordeed and Master of the Haegarand, wouldn't have returned to defeat him.'

'You're making this all come true, Lars – you're engineering it. What if I told you Halgoth is Hal Goth, an agent working in Para-technology? He's no more a Viking than I am.'

'All of us are not what we think we are, Nestatling. Maybe, you are not what you think you are?'

The strange dream of meeting Great Aunt Nellie in a white room chose that very moment to enter his head with a thump. 'You're Special Agent Nestat Montgomery, so do what you've been trained...' Nestat's musings were brought to an abrupt end when Halgoth woke up.

'Get my armour,' he bellowed, rising unsteadily to his feet. 'We're going to attack!'

Lars bowed and quickly left the room. Flonogson followed as fast as his limp would take him, leaving only Nestat, Halgoth and a lot of fish.

Halgoth went to a sink full of water, buried his head in it, roared a curse then shook his mane of hair like a wet dog. 'Now prove your worth, Nestatling, and give me council.'

As Nestat looked into Halgoth's wild eyes he realised how much he wished Hal Goth was standing in front of him. For the first time in many years he felt a pang of hurt in his heart; he'd lost a friend.

'The light is fading fast; this will help us. I suggest a feint at the main door whilst we attack where the monorail enters a tunnel.'

'A what?' said Halgoth.

'There's a tunnel, a kind of back door to the fortress.' Nestat realised he'd have to keep this simple; Hal of Paratech had long gone.

'A back entrance?' said Halgoth, spraying spittle. 'I'll not creep about like some cowardly night-crawling sneak-thief. We attack the front!'

Nestat wasn't about to disagree. 'Very well, Lord Halgoth. We attack the front. We'll keep in mind the back door should the battle go ill.'

'That is good council,' said Halgoth. 'I will inspect my army now.'

Lars entered the room clad in mail and helm with a sword hanging from his belt. Draped over one arm hung another mail coat, this one very bright and ornate; in the other hand he held a horned helm edged with gold. Nestat stepped to the side-lines and watched Halgoth being attired. When the last touches had been made, the giant Viking drew his sword and, marching towards the door, roared, 'Leg Cobbler will not find rest until it has drunk deeply on blood. Follow me!'

They followed, through the restaurant and into the cold Icelandic evening.

Nestat couldn't restrain a gasp of amazement. It appeared the whole village had turned out, all in full armour, carrying axes, spears, swords, round shields and flaming torches. In the centre of the throng was a battering ram with an iron ram's head.

Flonogson, sitting in a chair on the restaurant patio and not wearing warlike apparel, held a steaming mug with both hands. He took a sip, winked at Nestat and said, 'Good luck – you'll need it. Bloody nutters.'

Nestat ignored him, but the words drove home. 'Are the flaming torches really necessary?' he whispered to Lars. 'They'll see us a mile off.'

'Lord Halgoth commanded them,' said Lars.

Nestat didn't say anything, but if the Hal of old had been right about Baron Von Sheit then a bloodbath was about to ensue. If he were to have a chance of saving Hal and killing Slash he had to make for the tunnel the first chance he got. He held on to this thought for dear life amid the madness of the moment.

Halgoth raised the point of his sword to the heavens. 'Odin!'

The crowd in turn shouted, 'Odin!'

With Nestat following, Halgoth walked through his troops towards Baron Von Sheit's fortress. The Flurdeburdekull army closed in behind and the assault on the invisible volcano began.

LIBER NIGELLUS
THURSDAY EVENING

'Ah, Margot, please come in,' said The Baron, rising from his chair behind the desk.

De Witte stepped over the threshold into the rock-hewn chamber and instantly forgot the unpleasant smell emanating from an Ottoman by the door. The reason was a huge glass tank occupying a considerable part of the room.

'Everyone is here,' said The Baron. 'Well almost everyone. Your father will be joining us shortly.'

She acknowledged Slash standing next to the desk, with Spank squatting on the floor alongside, but her gaze returned to the tank and something floating about in the green liquid inside.

'My wife, Margot,' said The Baron with sadness, 'and the reason for needing the book.'

The distant sound of an air raid siren cranking up broke the exchange.

'Please excuse me a moment, will you?' The Baron pressed a green button on a monitor. 'My my, we appear to have company.'

'What's that?' said Slash.

'The villagers are about to attack my headquarters. Not to worry, though.' He pressed a red button. 'Are the men fully armed and ready, Hauptsturmführer?'

'Yes, sir,' came a reply.

'Is there any need for concern?'

'None whatsoever, sir.'

'Good. Then deal with it.' He pressed the button again and looked at De Witte. 'Now where were we? Ah yes, do you have the book?'

She patted her bag. 'Of course, but until I see my father it stays inside. Are you under attack?'

'No need to concern yourself, Margot, just a minor inconvenience from ignorant locals with pitchforks and scythes.'

Her gut feeling was Nestat was behind this, that he'd made it, that he'd soon be joining her. She could hardly suppress a smile. 'Why is your wife in a fish tank?'

The Baron lost his aloof manner and rubbed his legs with agitation. 'She, she wasn't well and – and she succumbed to her illness – and, and I had to preserve her in special fluid – and–'

'You shot her,' said Slash without emotion.

'Oh, Wilberforce, must you be so cruel?'

'Well it's true.'

De Witte shook her head slowly in disbelief. 'You shot your wife?'

'By accident,' The Baron whined. 'A bit like your father.'

'Not now, you idiot,' said Slash.

'What?' said De Witte coldly.

The Baron sat back in the chair and buried his face in his hands.

Slash took over. 'You see, Margot, he can't help shooting things – unless you have a lover or sweetheart, that is. He doesn't shoot anything that has an emotional attachment to a living entity, but–'

'I'm safe then,' she said, her thoughts momentarily

drifting to Nestat. Then reality caught her with a left hook. 'He shot my father?'

'Yes, but I was about to say—'

She looked at The Baron. 'Did you?'

The Baron looked up. 'I'm sorry, Margot. My finger slipped, but we—'

The news provoked anger, not grief. 'Then I'm going to destroy the book.' She began to turn the clasp on the bag.

'No!' both men shouted together.

'I was about to say he'll live,' said Slash.

Her fingers stopped. 'He'll live – what are you saying?'

'We can bring him back,' said Slash. 'The book can bring him back, and The Baron's wife. That's why we needed the book in the first place.'

'The book can bring...' her words trailed off as a rear door to the chamber opened and a blue suit entered, pushing a trolley on which lay a body shape under a white sheet.

'You see,' said The Baron, his face brightening. 'I told you your father would be joining us shortly. You'll have him in your arms in no time. But we must have the book, Margot.'

De Witte remembered flicking through the pages on the plane. There was definitely something weird and dark about the book. Could it hold magical power? Could they return her father to the living?'

'Are you saying you can bring my father back to life?'

'Yes,' said both men together.

'Seriously?'

They nodded.

Her fingers began working the clasp again, only this time in the correct sequence. A hiss of air came from the bag as she opened it, causing both men to gasp, but reaching inside she took out the intact book with one hand and a gun with the other. 'I hope for both your sakes this works.'

The Baron leant over the desk and was about to press a yellow button when De Witte cautioned, 'I wouldn't if I were you,' as she levelled the gun at his head.

'I'd do as she says,' said Slash.

Withdrawing his hand, The Baron chuckled and replaced his monocle. 'You have great spirit, Margot. I admire that. Do you like volcanoes, because there's always a place for a—'

'Shall we get on with it?' Slash interrupted.

'Yes, of course.' The Baron beckoned the blue suit to bring the trolley over. 'Now give the book to the doctor, Margot.'

De Witte walked forward and placed it on the desk, never once lowering the gun.

The instant Slash picked it up she noticed the same look on his face she'd seen on the airship: covetous hunger.

The blue suit parked the trolley next to the desk and left.

She glanced down at the shape beneath the sheet. Was this really possible? Grief caused a tear to track down her cheek, but anger kept her finger firmly on the trigger.

Slash opened the book, flicked through some pages and stopped about halfway in. He silently mouthed words then said, 'This is it. Spank, up on the desk, now!'

Spank looked up but didn't move.

'It's alright, nothing to worry about,' he said in a softer tone. 'You'll be getting it back soon.' He reinforced his words by pulling aside the folds of the cloak and revealing the withered arm hanging on a string from his neck.

Spank chattered and did what he was told.

The Baron looked on eagerly.

De Witte's gun traced an arc between The Baron and Slash.

Slash leant over the trolley and began chanting words from the book. Most were unintelligible, but De Witte managed to pick up a few: gypsy, porridge, monkey,

Pythagoras, Conan Doyle. Then his voice, which had been monotone until now, began to crescendo. He suddenly grabbed Spank by the foot, held him upside down and shook him, shouting above the screeching primate, 'Let life return!'

Spank broke free, ran to the tank and climbed on top, chattering and baring his teeth in anger.

The three of them stared at the trolley.

For a while nothing happened. But then something twitched under the sheet, a finger.

De Witte screamed and all three of them jumped back as the sheet flew off and Forest De Witte III leapt up. The thin old man stood motionless, swaying from side to side, his vacant eyes staring at the wall.

'Daddy?' De Witte ventured.

She recoiled as he turned to face her. His head wobbled as if on a spring, and stuck in a hole in his temple was a cork from a wine bottle, which wasn't doing a good job preventing something leaking. With an idiotic grin, he walked towards her like a marionette in the hands of a drunken puppeteer.

'What have you done to him?' she yelled, backing away.

Slash frantically began thumbing through pages in the book.

'Daddy! Daddy! What have they done to you?'

Forest responded by rolling his eyes back into his head.

'Is this what is going to happen to mein liebchen?' said The Baron, horrified.

'I must have missed something,' said Slash.

'Stop it. Stop it. Stop it, Do something, Slash.' said Margot De Witte.

'Hold on a moment,' said Slash. 'Aha! That's it! Spank – get over here quickly.'

Forest De Witte, his long fingers snapping like an angry crab, continued towards her.

The Baron drew his Luger and began shooting at Mr De Witte, who absorbed every bullet, moving with an increasingly unorthodox gait.

Margot's back hit the wall. Forest stopped. One eye righted itself in its socket. He opened his mouth as if to speak. Margot closed her eyes. She felt his body brush past and heard the door open and close. She opened her eyes – her fear turned to anger.

'Get him back,' yelled Slash. 'I can fix him. Spank, will you get over here, now!'

The Baron pressed a black button and gave instructions to security to apprehend a wayward zombie.

Margot De Witte marched purposefully towards The Baron, only stopping when her gun was inches from his head.

He winced and turned away.

'Don't,' said Slash. 'I got a bit of the ritual wrong. I can make him normal.'

'That *thing* isn't my father,' she said, keeping her eyes on The Baron. 'Make it quick, Slash.'

'The answer was here all along, on the first page.'

She remembered her reaction to the gothic image of a demon when opening the book. 'You have to cut off the monkey's head?'

'Yes,' said Slash. 'The head is used to reanimate. The paw is used for–'

Spank screeched from on top of the tank. A trap door opened above him and a bamboo pole came down, followed by three monkeys. Spank's terror and rage changed to a shriek of delight as he met his estranged family.

The red button on The Baron's desk flashed blue.

'Spank,' yelled Slash. 'Get over here this instant!'

'May I answer that?' said The Baron.

De Witte nodded.

He pressed the button. Gunfire and angry voices came over the speakers. 'Are you there, sir?'

'What's going on?'

'They're tougher than we thought. We've shut the steel

door but they've got a battering ram.'

'Why haven't you shot them all?' said The Baron angrily.

'The bullets don't have much effect. I think they're wearing body armour.'

'Since when did armour stop bullets?'

'I mean modern stuff – Kevlar. You'll have to do something.'

'Very well, I will. Get ready for you know what.'

'Yes, sir.'

The Baron faced the bank of switches on the desk, the ones with ancient Icelandic under each one and Post-it notes beneath. He selected Grosser Blitzkrieg mitt extras and flicked the switch. A dull rumbling from deep beneath their feet immediately followed.

Spank gesticulated to his family and pointed at The Baron. They all started gibbering and chattering.

Slash threw a venomous glance at Spank. 'I'm going to chop up your arm and eat it with broccoli unless you come here now!'

En famille, the monkeys proceeded to fling poo at him.

The Baron's face was ashen as he mumbled, 'Mein Gotte, not again.'

'What did you say?' said De Witte, feeling the floor move.

'Witherspoon and Smythe used ancient Icelandic on the switches – thought it more in keeping. I can't read ancient Icelandic, that's why I told them to put Post-it notes underneath.'

She shrugged. 'So?'

'I flicked the wrong switch once before, some years ago. It caused all sorts of trouble.'

'What have you done now, Hardinger?' said Slash.

'One of the cleaners must have mixed them up,' he whined.

'I don't understand,' said De Witte.

'It means I've flicked Gute Nacht Vienna and the

volcano is about to erupt.'

De Witte backed off and stood in front of the tank, her gun trained on The Baron.

Slash quickly grabbed the book from the desk, stepped away and drew a gun.

The Baron snapped the clip into his Luger and pointed it at De Witte.

LOVE'S LABOUR'S LOST
THURSDAY NIGHT, KNIGHTSBRIDGE

Tommy watched the goons leave the suite and didn't move until the doors closed on the lift. He walked to the suite, slipped a hand inside his jacket and switched on the power to a battery pack. Sir Hector's frantic pleas were still coming over the earphone when he pushed the door open and walked in. 'Don't worry, he won't hurt you.'

Sir Hector went bug-eyed. 'Boyle – Thomas Boyle?'

The Viscotti brothers acknowledged him with a nod.

'Thanks guys,' said Tommy, 'I reckon he's squirmed enough.'

The brothers put their weapons away, and as they left Vincenzo said, 'We hang around outside for a bit, just in case, eh?'

'Great – thanks.'

'Hi, Tom,' said Vicky.

'Hi, gorgeous, you did a great job.'

Sven began to slide down the wall.

'And you, buddy,' said Tommy, 'couldn't have done it without your help.'

Sven grinned inanely.

Tommy gestured to Vicky. 'Give him a hand will you.

This is between me and my old boss.'

She helped Sven to his feet and led him out, closing the door behind her.

Sir Hector stepped backwards, grabbed the back of one of many chairs surrounding the large table and sat down heavily. He mouthed a few words but no sound accompanied them.

'Well, well,' said Tommy. 'You appear to be lost for words. Not like you were with the press when you stitched me up on that insider trading charge.'

'Boyle – all this is *your* doing?'

'Yep, just a little game. Much like the one you've played with my friends.'

Sir Hector pocketed Vicky's mobile and glared defiantly. 'You're not having it. And don't think of trying to rough me up, I'm quite capable of looking after myself you know.'

'Don't be silly.' He took an iPhone from a pocket and tapped it. 'The mobile was a ruse – stopped you checking too closely. The wire in her bra wasn't just support. He touched the screen of the phone, 'This baby has everything I need.'

'You bastard!'

'That's rich coming from you. You sacked me, sullied my name and nearly got me put in prison. You had me contemplating suicide, and all to cover up your own dirty dealings, and I don't mean that kinky re-enactment of the battle of Waterloo.'

'What do you want, money, because there isn't any in that case over there?'

'I banked on it.'

'What?'

'You see I banked on a great many things with you, Sir Hector Chisholm. Let me go through them, just for the record. First: I knew you'd see through my friend's private detective impersonation and realise his story was daft.'

'Who could fail to notice that?'

'Right,' agreed Tommy. 'Second: saying only he and the girl knew about your indiscretion was sure to get you doing what you do best, turning the tables and frightening people. My buddy didn't know the real plan so once you had the upper hand he wasn't acting anymore.'

'That was rather cruel of you, Boyle.'

'Only to be kind. He's a good friend, and hopefully this will stop him playing games before something nasty *really* happens to him one day. Third: after all this it was simply a question of time and location. Sven, who you know as Farlow, was able to communicate that to Vicky, who you've just met.'

'And the men with guns?'

Tommy smiled. 'Not family, obviously, but they're for real, unlike Professional Cleaning Services. Companies that offer bodyguards in the public domain don't carry real guns.'

'How do you know about them?' he said with surprise.

Tommy's smile broke into a chuckle. 'Everybody in the company knows about *them* and how you use *them* to scare people you want to walk over. I'm surprised I didn't get a visit; then again, I went down without a fight. I'm making up for that now.'

Sir Hector sneered and said grudgingly, 'All very clever. So you want money, revenge, is that it?'

'You really don't get it, do you? I don't want a penny of your rotten money, or revenge. The hooker in question doesn't even know any of this has happened. She's most likely not the sharpest knife in the drawer otherwise she could have held you to ransom herself. But she isn't, so you needn't worry on that score – to her you're just another rich twat who laid out cash for a kinky screw. Unless I make a phone call, that is.'

'Then what *do* you want?'

'I want my name back, and I want it back as clean as it was before you set me up.'

'All this was to get your reputation cleared?'

Tommy tapped the iPhone again. 'With this as leverage to make certain you do the right thing – yes. Once I see an apology in the papers, including the offer of my job back, then all of this will be history.'

'You want your job back?' he blustered. 'You were good but–'

'Don't worry, I'll decline.'

'Oh, will you?' Sir Hector looked more puzzled than ever.'

'The stock market and I are no longer friends. But that doesn't mean I'm going to be remembered as a cheat.'

'That's all well and good, but how can I clear you without compromising myself?'

'Oh come on, you and junior managed to cover your tracks hacking into my account.'

'Don't involve my son in this; he knew nothing.'

The words hit Tommy like a punch in the face. 'Are you serious?'

'He plays straight, Boyle. Takes after his Mother.'

'Does he?' Tommy made a huge effort and regained his inner composure. 'Then all the more reason to keep this quiet. Look, I don't care how you do it so long as it doesn't involve dumping it on some other poor sod's lap. New information has come to light; how could it have been overlooked? Create a fictitious proxy in the Hong Kong office and say he vanished, something like that. Use your imagination.'

Sir Hector began to bite one of his well-manicured nails.

'I'll give you three days, no longer. If I don't see it in the Sunday papers then I'm paying a visit to Lady Chisholm and the media first thing Monday morning.'

Sir Hector stopped biting his nail and nodded vigorously.

'Good. I'll leave it with you.'

As Tommy turned to leave, Sir Hector said, 'How *did* you find out about me and that prostitute?'

'Believe it or not, pure chance. Then again, maybe the Almighty does take up the cause of the innocent against the wicked. That's worth consideration when you try to screw someone over next time, don't you think? Oh, and I guess you'll want to destroy *your* recording of this evening. Good bye, Sir Hector, and I hope we never meet again.'

*

Tommy closed the door to the suite and exhaled loudly.

'Everything go okay?' Vincenzo asked as they all walked to the lift.

'Yeah, thanks, boys. I owe you big time.'

'No problem,' said Michael. 'Danny says you're always nice to him. You're family now. You come round one day and we all have lunch together. His missus cooks a great Chow Mein.'

As they waited for the lift, he said to Vicky and Sven, 'I'll see you tomorrow. Thank you both so much.'

'I did okay?' asked Sven, still shell-shocked.

'Brilliantly.'

'I thought everything had gone wrong?' He leant forward and whispered, 'And *who are* these guys'

'I'll tell you tomorrow,' Tommy whispered back.

'What about me?' said Vicky.

'You were the consummate professional.' Tommy leant forward to kiss her on the cheek but she turned her head and their lips made contact. He pulled back quickly. 'Sorry, I didn't mean to—'

'Forget it.' The lift doors opened. 'Are you coming down with us?'

'No, I'll use the stairs, just in case Penny sees us. Bye for now.'

Tommy watched the doors close, then walked to the stairs. Penny would be waiting.

*

Tommy sat down and smiled at Penny. Struggling not to sound smug, he said, 'Well, still think I'm a liar and a cheat?'

She swallowed a mouthful of pudding. 'I thought you were never coming back. Can I take this thing out for a bit, it's making my ear sore?'

Tommy was taken aback by her under-reaction. 'Yes, of course you can but—'

'Tell me when to put it back in.'

'What?'

'But it had better be soon because I'll have to leave shortly.'

Tommy put both his hands on his head and stared at her.

'Is something wrong?'

'Didn't you hear anything?'

She bit her lip and shook her head.

He pulled the battery pack out of the inside pocket. It must have been *on* all along. He hadn't switched it *on* upstairs, he'd switched it *off*.

'I don't believe it!'

'It's all over then?' she said quietly.

'Yes.'

'Did everything go okay?'

'Yes.'

'So you proved your innocence?'

'It'll be in the Sunday papers.'

'Tommy, that's wonderful news,' she beamed. 'You can pick up the pieces and get on with your life now.'

He swallowed hard. 'But I wanted *you* to hear what happened, Penny.'

'It doesn't matter. What's important is you were telling the truth.' She paused. 'I'm sorry I doubted you. It must have been awful. Please forgive me.'

'Of course I forgive you.'

'Thank you. I won't tell Hector, I'll let him read about it on Sunday. It'll be a nice surprise for him.'

'A nice surprise?' said Tommy, astounded.

'He doesn't like cheats, but always admits when he's wrong. I wouldn't be surprised if he called you to apologise.'

Unable to find words, Tommy bowed his head.

'I hope the person who did this to you will get their comeuppance,' said Penny.

'I doubt it,' he mumbled at the tablecloth. 'Doesn't this change things between us, Penny?'

'You mean as in – us? Us as in – as we were?'

Tommy looked up and nodded.

'This isn't easy to say but – well – I love Hector.'

He gulped. It felt like his insides had been ripped out. 'You love him?'

'We had some great times, Tommy. You're a nice guy, that's why I stuck with you all those months, hoping you'd snap out. Well, now you have at last and I'm happy for you, more so because you've shown you are the straight guy I always hoped you were. But laughs and sex aren't enough. I realised that some months ago. It would never have worked.'

'Are you going to marry him?'

She shrugged. 'If he asked, yes, I think I would.'

'Oh, Penny. All this was for you.' Tommy felt close to tears.

'I'm sorry,' she said quietly.

The clink of cutlery in the background became louder as he stared at the uneaten meal in front of him.

Penny glanced at her watch and stood. 'I must go. I'll get a cab, don't worry.'

'Okay.'

'How's the book coming along, by the way?'

'Almost finished,' he said, faking a smile.

'That's great! I look forward to reading it when it's published.'

She came around the table and kissed him on the forehead, her lips lingering longer than they need have. He felt the warmth in her gesture, but it was more like motherly affection. It had all been for nothing.

VALHALLA BECKONS
THURSDAY NIGHT, ICELAND

Making no attempt to blend into the melee of men holding tight formation on their climb up the volcano, Halgoth, well out in front, sang at the top of his voice a Nordic war chant. The Flurdeburdekull army kept rhythm by smashing swords and spears against their large round shields. Nestat could hardly believe the contrast between Hal and this wild man, who seemed oblivious to danger as he led the deafening racket.

Nestat walked a little way behind the warlord, keeping his eyes peeled and his wits about him, expecting bullets to start flying any minute, but so far nothing, in spite of the flaming torches and noise announcing their progress on the tortuous climb. He began to think maybe The Baron had decided to vacate via the tunnel and monorail, then hundreds of silhouettes appeared on a ridge in front of them.

Halgoth concluded his chant with a blood-curdling scream and raised an arm, bringing the army to a clattering halt. In the following silence, he glared into the darkness at his shadowy adversaries, appearing to take stock in preparation for the next move. It didn't take long. He drew his sword and shouted, 'Odin.'

Nestat didn't have a chance to sidestep as with a deafening 'Odin' the army began its onslaught, carrying him along with it. Then the bullets *did* start flying.

He heard them hitting armour with pinging ricochets and thumping direct hits, but amazingly they kept on running and only one or two of the villagers fell. He stayed behind a particularly large man to shield himself from flying lead.

The battering ram rumbled along as the warriors came to close quarters with Von Sheit's men.

Halgoth fought like a man possessed, which of course he was, and the body count quickly stacked up.

Nestat shot a few men but wanted to keep most of his ammunition for Slash, at least five shots. He wrested an assault rifle from the tight clasp of a dead man and began opening up with it.

Lars ran past and took a hit dead centre that threw him back on his feet. Nestat expected him to go down, but he shook himself and launched back into the fray.

Puzzled, he managed to get alongside the restaurant owner and shouted above the din, 'What kind of armour is that you're wearing, it's amazing.'

'Kevlar under the mail,' Lars replied, swiping a head off with an axe.

'Is Kevlar mentioned in a saga, Lars?'

'Ya, the eBay saga.'

Nestat laughed. 'I didn't see you putting it on Halgoth.'

'He's invincible; he doesn't need it.'

Nestat felt a cold hand grip his heart. It would be a miracle if Halgoth hadn't been shot already. He looked about but couldn't see his six-foot seven body anywhere, so he made for where he had last seen him fighting. It didn't take long to discoverer that miracles didn't feature in this saga.

Halgoth lay on the ground with a few warriors in attendance. The noise of battle faded into the distant background for Nestat as he knelt next to him.

'Ah, Nestatling,' he gasped. 'The battle goes well?'

Nestat felt a lump come to his throat. His friend, who somewhere dwelt within this body, was dying. 'It goes well,' he said.

Halgoth coughed up blood. 'You must slay Harold, Nestatling. Use your plan, the one you told me of.'

'I will.'

'My eyes grow dim. I am pierced by many arrows.'

Nestat didn't think it appropriate to mention they were bullets.

'Give me my sword,' said Halgoth.

Nestat reached out, grabbed *Leg Cobbler* from where it lay next to a pile of heads, and placed the hilt in Halgoth's bloody hand.

'What do you see, Nestatling?'

Nestat looked to the men around Halgoth for a clue of what he should be seeing.

One got the idea, made a few shapes with his hands and mouthed, 'A Viking ship.'

With this, and drawing on his knowledge of Icelandic history, Nestat said, 'Valhalla beckons, Halgoth, and Odin's hall awaits you. I see a Viking ship on the clouds.'

'What are you on about, Nestat? What the hell's happened?'

'Hal?'

'Flippin' heck, something hurts.'

'You're back!' Nestat was ecstatic. 'Hang on. Don't give up.' He turned to one of the men and yelled, 'Get help, quickly.'

'Nestat – I'm frightened.'

Nestat turned back to his friend and held him gently by the shoulders. 'Don't be. Hold on.'

Hal's words trailed into an almost inaudible whisper, his eyelids flickered a few times, then, the crystalline blue eyes stared lifelessly at the sky.

'Hal!'

Nestat remained kneeling with his head lowered as the battle raged about them.

'Vengeance will be ours, Hal. Now I have two people to kill.' He stood and wiped away tears.

A phalanx of blue suits roared over a ridge on quad bikes, from the direction of the tunnel. Most fell to a hail of arrows, but one, possibly thinking suicide wasn't part of his employment contract, turned tail and began to head back the way he'd come.

Without thinking, Nestat grabbed the rifle from the ground and put it to his shoulder. He held the biker in the crosshairs. It was a long shot for a moving target. He fired, and for a second he thought he'd missed, until the quad veered off to one side and hit a rock, catapulting the rider high in the air. Dropping the rifle, Nestat ran over, pulled the bike back onto its wheels and roared off.

A few minutes and he arrived at the docking mast and airship then followed the monorail. The tunnel came into view as a bright light piercing the darkness. He sped through the open steel doors and into the volcano, stopping some hundreds of metres later where a train stood next to a platform.

It appeared all of The Baron's men had been committed to battle as he hadn't met a soul, until now. A blue suit stood under a sign saying, "Entrance to Evil Headquarters", staring at him in amazement, a gun hanging limp in his hand.

'I know I look a state, old chap, but there's a war going on out there.'

The blue suit was patently confused by Nestat's muddy tuxedo and his cultured non-Icelandic accent.

'W-who ... W-what ...'

A dull rumble deep in the heart of the Volcano and the sound of creaking metal was followed by a fall of rocks from above. This was enough for the blue suit to drop his gun and run.

Nestat dodged through the hail of rocks to the

entrance and followed signs in the tunnel leading the way to Baron Von Sheit's office. He'd only gone a short distance when he encountered an old man wobbling toward him at pace. Nestat aimed the gun but a bullet wasn't necessary. Seemingly oblivious to his presence, the man passed by and continued bouncing off the walls in the direction of the station. The rumbling and vibrations grew stronger.

Five minutes later and Nestat stood outside a door with 'Baron Von Sheit' written on it in gold letters. He took a moment to catch his breath and compose himself. A shudder racked him as a terrible feeling of imminent death gripped his innards, he could almost smell it. Gathering all his resolve, and with a grim expression, he threw the door open.

The monocle and duelling scar instantly identified Baron Von Sheit. The Luger in his podgy hand pointed at Margot De Witte.

Margot stood in front of a huge glass tank, looking as beautiful as ever. She offered a wan smile of welcome whilst keeping a gun pointed at The Baron.

And there, at last, was Slash, unmistakable in his Lycra shellsuit and lead-soled diver's boots, one higher than the other. In one hand he held the book, in the other a gun, pointing at him.

Nestat ground his teeth as he aimed the weapon at Slash's head. But a vague, blurry movement, just within lateral vision, stole his attention. Without altering his stance, he glanced towards Margo and the tank.

A body had floated into view behind her, and like an angel of death with outstretched arms it drifted in the greenish liquid. Tendrils of yellowed, tattered fabric caressed the glass. As though moved by some unseen current, they twisted and probed like ghostly fingers exploring a way out. The bug-eyes and bloated features reminded him of something: a school biology class, a bottled frog in formaldehyde for dissection, maybe? – or the grisly trophies of Evandor Vine the Viennese Eviscerator in his lair at Basingstoke, possibly?

Then a horrible sickness gripped his stomach as realisation forced itself into his reluctant mind: a dark mole just to the right of the top lip; a small tattoo of a dove above the left ankle.

'Sally!'

'Indeed it is,' said The Baron. 'It appears we have a Stalingrad standoff.'

'Mexican,' Margot corrected.

'Not where I come from. Agent Montgomery, I presume,' said The Baron casting a quick glance at Nestat.

'That's my fiancée in there,' said Nestat.

'No, that's my wife in there. Shoot him, Wilberforce.'

'With pleasure,' said Slash.

Four guns fired simultaneously.

Slash might have hit Nestat if Spank hadn't reached down from the top of the tank and grabbed the book.

Nestat's bullet would definitely have made contact if Slash hadn't moved to grab the monkey.

Margot would have hit The Baron if she hadn't turned her gun on Slash to protect Nestat.

The Baron didn't miss.

Spank threw the book into the air.

Slash clutched his side with one hand where Margot's bullet had hit, dropped the gun from the other and managed to catch the book, only to let it slide through the unravelling bandages on his hand.

Nestat fired again.

'No!' screamed Slash as the bullet hit the side of his cheek. 'I must be holding the book. I must be holding the book. Give me the book. Tell him, Margot.'

Margot stared down at a widening red stain on her chest. 'Kill him, Nestat.' She strained to smile then collapsed.

The Baron pointed his gun at Nestat and said with desperation, 'Don't kill him, Montgomery, I need him.'

Margot unsteadily raised her gun and fired, sending the Baron's gun flying from his hand.

Nestat walked up to Slash, held the gun inches from his head and pulled the trigger until the breech locked back. Five shots to the face.

The Baron howled in despair, 'Woe! Oh woe is me!' and fell with great theatrical melancholy to the floor.

De Witte dragged herself towards Nestat.

The office began to shake violently, and a small leak in the tank, where the bullet that passed through De Witte had hit the glass, suddenly became a big leak. Cracks began radiating away from the hole, accompanied by sharp snapping sounds.

The Baron screamed as he shuffled on his knees to the tank.

'Nestat, Nestat,' said Margot in a weak voice.

He continued to stare at Slash's erstwhile face, her voice slowly filtering into his sweet moment of vengeance. He turned towards the whispered words. 'Margot!' A smeared trail of blood tracked her desperate effort to reach him. 'Margot! please, not you.' He knelt and cradled her head in his lap.

She reached into his jacket and put something in one of the pockets. 'Keep it safe and remember me.'

'I'm getting you out of here,' he said.

'It's too late. I love you, Nestat. I'll always love you.' She closed her eyes.

For the second time that evening, Nestat felt the unfamiliar sensation of tears coursing down his cheeks. The room was falling to bits around him, but he didn't care. The sound of cascading water and a yelp drew his attention to The Baron, just in time to see him enveloped by thousands of gallons of green liquid and the body of Sally, to which he clung for dear life as they were swept across the floor.

'Mien liebchen,' he wailed as they came to rest. He lifted one of her arms only for it to come away from her body with a squelch. He howled in anguish, a fissure opened up in the floor sending smoke and sparks flying into the room, and The Baron and Sally vanished into the fiery chasm.

Nestat had seen enough. The ingrained survival instinct kicked in. He gently eased De Witte's head onto the floor, kissed her pale forehead and then ran for the door, followed by four terrified monkeys, one carrying a withered arm.

Nestat stopped and looked down at the monkeys. 'Come on,' he said, 'let's get out of here, if we can.'

LAST FLIGHT TO NOWHERE
THURSDAY, CLOSE TO MIDNIGHT, ICELAND

'Do you mind if I sit next to you?' said a woman's voice

Nestat didn't open his eyes; his troubled thoughts were in Von Sheit's office: Slash dead and revenge exacted, Sally falling to bits in a rush of preserving fluid, Margot in a pool of blood and The Baron and the remains of his fiancé falling into a fiery crevasse. Being polite would come as a welcome distraction.

'Please, be my guest.'

'That's very kind of you,' she said.

A soft Irish lilt, which combined with the faint smell of Frankincense and rustling capacious fabric, confirmed the profession of his companion-to-be on the flight.

'You're a nun,' he said.

'You guessed without opening your eyes. I saw that. Ah, that's very clever, yes, very clever.'

'Not really, and I would have preferred a priest.'

'You need to confess, my child.'

'No, I need to hit someone.'

'Oh dear me, you're a one.'

Nestat heard another sound. Anyone but a nun would instantly have thrown him on guard. His heavy lids parted.

163

No, it was just a nun fiddling with something in her robes. She jumped slightly on seeing him looking at her.

'I'm having a little trouble with the clip – eh – the clip on my sacraments case,' she said.

Nestat smiled. 'You have good taste in perfume, Sister..?'

'Sister Winnett, sir.'

'Poison by Christian Dior?'

'Your sense of smell is as keen as your guesswork, Mr..?'

'Nestat Montgomery.'

'Nestat Montgomery. What a nice name, very unusual.'

'Thank you.'

'Are you on business in Ireland, Mr Montgomery, or having a holiday?'

'This plane is going to Ireland?'

He'd bought a ticket for the first flight out of Iceland. In a daze, all he'd heard was 'credit card' and 'leaving immediately before the volcano closes the airport'. It had been a last call, a mad dash to the plane, lax security in the panic and quite unlike a dignified saunter to a first class seat, his travelling norm. The last thing he'd seen as he ran for the gate was the monkeys sneaking onto the baggage cart.

Sister Winnett took out a knife with a death's head on the hilt and began to peel a grapefruit.

'That's a strange object for a bride of Christ to possess.'

'I've never been that keen on apples; it's the pips.'

'I meant the knife?'

'Ah yes, my fruit knife; it was a gift from his Holiness the Pope.'

'He gives gifts like that?'

'So I believe.'

'So you believe?'

Sister Winnett wriggled her bottom. 'Well, his Holiness didn't give it to *me* exactly; his accountant did when I strung ... I mean, when I met him on a bridge in Rome one time. He told me it had been a gift from his Holiness. That was shortly before I – well – it's not important. Would you care for a segment?'

Nestat declined.

The plane taxied, howled down the runway and they were airborne. Glancing out the window he saw ash clouds beginning to obscure the city lights below and wondered how Lars and the people of Flurdeburdekull were coping with yet another eruption. No doubt putting it down to a giant dragon, he guessed. A stiff drink beckoned. He pressed the flight attendant button.

Sister Winnett had finished the grapefruit and was pawing over the safety sheet. A calloused, nicotine stained right forefinger drew his attention to her hand. About to comment, the arrival of the stewardess stopped him.

'What can I be after getting you, top of the mornin', yah?'

The young woman's smiling face beneath a bun of blonde hair clearly said Scandinavian, but her melodic tone and jumble of accents didn't.

'I beg your pardon?'

'Will you be after wanting a drink, sur?'

'Yes, I'll have a gin and tonic.' He turned to the nun. 'Would you care for a drink, Sister?'

Still engrossed with the safety sheet, she shook her head.

Nestat smiled at the stewardess. 'Just for me then, Miss..?'

'Tove Murphy, and we don't have any gin.'

'A malt whisky then, no ice.'

'We don't serve alcohol. '

'What?'

'I can make you a nice cup of tea, yah?'

Nestat's eyes were drawn towards her feet, and a pair of very sensible black lace-up shoes not in keeping with her pink uniform. He then noticed they were exactly the same shoes as those worn by another nun and a basketball player across the aisle. Sister Winnett shared the same taste in footwear, as did a male flight attendant and three other passengers walking past.

'You're all wearing the same shoes,' he said. 'No alcohol, strange accent, what's going on here?'

Tove Murphy shook her head. 'Oh dear yah, I think he has rumbled us, Sister Winnett.'

Nestat's eyes widened. 'What do you mean *us*?' He felt a hand duck inside his jacket.

He spun his head to be greeted by the business end of his own gun.

'You're off to Knock, Mr. Montgomery,' said Sister Winnett. 'A miracle happened at Knock, did you know that?'

Nestat shook his head.

'Oh yes, and another is going to happen. Knock is going to be the new Rome, the new Vatican, and I'm going to be Pope. We've got an airport.'

Nestat found his voice. 'Nuns can't be popes, can they?'

'If Barbra Streisand can get into a Yeshiva then I can be Pope, alright!' She waved the gun dismissively. 'Anyway, that's just a minor technical detail. The bottom line is you picked the wrong plane, Mr. Montgomery. The passengers, Miss Murphy here and the captain and crew are an elite Hiberno-Scandinavian ecclesiastical hit team sent to establish a bridgehead at Knock. It began with a priest's vision of the Virgin Mary's socks. It's much bigger than that now.'

Nestat couldn't resist it, 'Let me guess, they've miraculously gone from size six to eight?'

'Don't mock us, Mr Montgomery.'

'Bigger than that – not size ten?'

'I'm warning you.'

'Big foot has been spotted in Ireland?'

Nestat didn't feel any pain as the bullet passed through his skull, just a brief micro-second of blissful peace before everything went white. The same couldn't be said for the occupants of the plane, as the bullet carried on through the opposite window. Three seats, a nun and a basketball player enlarged the hole considerably as they were sucked out, and the aircraft with its ecclesiastical hit team went into a steep dive towards the sea.

*

If anybody was paying particular attention, they would have observed four monkeys aboard improvised luggage-rafts paddling southwards away from the wreckage. But nobody was paying particular attention.

*

Agency chief, Frisbee Clench, folded his newspaper and placed it on the side of his desk. Sunlight streamed through the large sash window behind him, highlighting dust on a framed photograph of Nestat Montgomery shaking hands with the Prime Minister outside Number 10. He sighed and turned the picture face down.

His gaze shifted to the Slash/Baron Von Sheit file. He stared at it for some time, then picked up a rubber stamp and banged it down hard on the brown cardboard outer leaf – CLOSED, in red ink.

SLURP
FRIDAY MORNING, THE WEE HOURS, NOTTING HILL

'Finished,' said Tommy, hitting save on *Baron Von Sheit's Hedonistic Aquarium.* He shut the laptop, leant back and stretched.

Writing had kept the outside world away, stopped him from going over the events of the previous days in a destructive cycle of thought.

Penny didn't love him after all. She loved Gonzo ... she loved Hector. It didn't seem appropriate to call him Gonzo anymore.

'Things, Tommy Boyle,' he said, 'are never a bad as you think they are.'

A rap on the front door made him jump. He checked his watch: four thirty in the morning. Had Sir Hector changed his mind and hired some real thugs?

Another rap at the door.

Thugs don't rap, he reasoned, *they pound.* Nevertheless, he went to the kitchenette and took a large carving knife from a drawer. 'Who's there,' he said gruffly, a semi-tone lower than normal.

'It's me, Vicky.'

He threw back the dead-bolt and opened the door.

'Vicky! Great to see you but...' He trailed off, uncertain what to say next.

'I came on the off-chance. Penny's not here is she?'

'No.'

'It's just I thought you might be with her.'

'I'm home alone.'

'That's good. Well can I come in, or are you going to kill me?'

Tommy looked at the knife in his hand then put it on the side table next to the phone. 'Sorry, I had the jitters for a moment. Of course, come on in and sit down. Fancy a brew?'

'That'll be nice,' she said walking in and sitting on the sofa-bed.

Tommy flicked on the kettle. 'Give me your coat; I'll hang it up.'

He noticed she wore jeans and a loose sweater, not her normal working attire.

'Cheesewright is the only guy who calls at this time; I'm honoured. Thanks again for everything.'

'No problem.'

'I feel like I've pulled off a sting.'

'You did. Change a few names and put it in one of your books.'

'Yeah, right, although I'd be tempted to leave one in.' He shrugged. 'But that's over and I want to forget it, so I won't.' He wiped a couple of mugs. 'You've not been working tonight?'

'No. I took a break,' she said, quietly.

'Good move. All work and no play and all that.' He grinned. 'Or should I say the other way round?'

She didn't laugh. 'Don't, Tom, not now.'

'Hey, what's up?' he said, forgetting the tea and sitting next to her.

'It's what happened yesterday,' she said, close to tears.

Tommy's face contorted with anger. 'Has Chisholm done something? If he has I'll print and be damned!'

169

'No, it's nothing like that.'

'Then what? Tell me.'

She broke down.

He put his arms around her and held her tightly. She cried into his shoulder then pushed him away.

'I'm sorry, Vicky, I'm only trying to–'

'Why do you bother with me?'

'Me bother with you?' he said, astounded. 'Don't you mean the other way round?' He looked at her keenly. 'Do I detect a smidgeon of self-pity here?'

'Yes, you do. It's my turn.'

He couldn't suppress a chuckle. 'Fair enough, but let me put you straight. First off, you took me under your wing when I was a boring, self-centred drunk. Apart from you and Sven, everyone had given up on me, so don't give me that 'I'm not worth it' routine. You're my friend; I don't care what you do for a living. Second, you haven't asked me how it went with Penny.'

She snuffled and wiped her nose.

'I didn't win her back, Vicky. She dumped me once and for all time for Hector.'

'Oh, did she?'

'Yep. And going on what she said I reckon the wedding invites will be going out soon.'

'Oh. You, erm, don't seem upset.'

He shrugged. 'I was last night, but what can I do about it? It's a fact. I've given it my best shot and it didn't work, end of story.'

'So what now?' she said, sniffing and searching for a hanky.

Tommy went to the kitchenette, returned with some paper towels and sat down again. 'I'm taking your advice and ditching this bed-sit. I'm not going for something flash, just better. And I'm going to take a holiday before diving into my new job. That'll do for starters. And I've finished my book by the way.'

Vicky dabbed her eyes and smiled. 'Is it good; are you

happy with it?'

'Yeah, I reckon it's not bad. It's completely daft, though. I think it's what they call Marmite.'

'I like Marmite. Thanks, Tom.'

'What for?'

'For taking me the way I am.'

'Oh, Vicky, please.'

'I only do what I do because I have to.'

'You don't need to tell me anything.'

'I'm not going to – not yet. But trust me; it's not what I want.'

'I trust you more than anyone I know.' A thought popped into his head, a radical thought, and he was unsure what reaction he'd get. With the thought came a warm feeling, as if a sluice gate had started leaking something nice inside him.

He couldn't stop himself. 'Why don't you come on holiday with me, my treat and no hanky panky?' He raised his eyebrows. 'I'm going to the Caribbean.'

She answered by leaning over and kissing him. It was the kind of awkward first kiss that lovers talk about years later: a small bit of unexpected biting, the thrust and parry of tongues and noses as a rhythm sets in, a slurp where perhaps a slurp should not have been and, to finish, the melding of mouths in a silky and erotic exchange.

She broke off gently and said, 'Yes, I'll come.'

'Wow – you will? Are you sure?'

'Yeah, I'm sure. And when we get back ...'

'Yes?'

'If we don't utterly hate each other ...'

'Yes?'

'I might help you look for that new apartment.'

'Oh,' he said.

'Of course, I'll need a walk-in wardrobe and I read a lot so there will have to be a library.'

'Oh!' he said.

EPIPROLOGUE

Whiteness enveloped Nestat once more, only this time without the accompanying smells of herring; he never thought he'd miss something like that, but he did. Although unable to remember, he came to the conclusion the nun must have hit him on the head, but it hadn't hurt anywhere near as much as when Margot had whacked him. In fact he felt no pain at all. That was a real bonus.

Margot – dear Margot. He found out too late that she loved him, wanted him. Equally, he didn't realise he'd loved her until she lay dying on the floor in Sheit's office. Life was cruel: the unbearable shiteness of being mortal, of having a heart that could be wounded so deeply and yet continue to beat. He tried to put these thoughts on hold for now and concentrate on this moment in time. There would be an occasion for cathartic reflection, but this wasn't it.

He guessed that any second now Great Aunt Nellie would materialise, say something odd then fade away. Then he'd wake up somewhere or other and the process of picking up the pieces of real life would begin again.

A shape began to take human form, but *not* how it had been before. This time lots of shapes began to appear, surrounding him. The whiteness dissipated, and with clarity came shock. Sitting on a sea of cold, white marble, he looked up at what were familiar faces, not one of them Great Aunt Nellie.

'Hello, Nestat, I'm glad you're here,' said Halgoth.

Looking down at him, and dressed in full armour, stood Halgoth, Warlord of the Beordeed and Master of the Haegarand, but the voice belonged to Hal Goth of Para-tech.

'This can't be happening,' said Nestat,

'What can't be happening?' said Hal

'You're not happening. You can't be real. There are no bullet holes.'

'Bullet holes, what you on about?'

'I saw you die, Halg– Hal.'

'You're joking, aren't you?' said Hal, looking worried and confused at the same time. 'Why am I dressed like this? I haven't done something *really* bad, have I?'

'Are you real?'

'Stop larking about, Nestat.'

Nestat pointed at a figure approaching from behind Hal. 'And Margot, is *she* real?'

'I hope so,' she said, trying to smile but not quite managing it. 'We all seem to have arrived here at much the same time. Is it some kind of dungeon?'

She was asking *him*? Nestat shook his head; the words wouldn't come. He looked about as he struggled unsteadily to his feet. 'Smythe, Witherspoon, Stodey – you as well, MacGrip?'

'Hello Master Montgomery,' said MacGrip, facing someone else.

Lars the Icelandic restaurateur stepped forward. 'It appears, after all, that I'm not the only one who isn't what I thought I was, Nestatling.'

Then Nestat saw The Baron dragging his feet despondently towards them from another part of the room. The room: a massive, white space, of inestimable length, of indiscernible height, filled with hundreds, maybe thousands of people – people as far as the eye could see.

'This can't be happening,' said Nestat. The room spun. 'It can't. It can't.'

He closed his eyes, hoping to blank out the madness and awake perhaps in some sane death.

'It is never easy,' said a blood-chillingly familiar wheezy voice, 'the first time around.'

Opening his eyes, Nestat instinctively reached for his gun, but found only a small book jammed in a pocket next to where it should have been. His arm fell limp at his side.

'You?'

Slash, appearing at ease with these surroundings, sashayed forward with a claw held out in a gesture of friendship. 'Welcome to The White Room, Nestat Montgomery.'

To be continued...

ALSO AVAILABLE FROM
PILLAR INTERNATIONAL PUBLISHING

The Young Dictator
By
Rhys Hughes

Last Orders at the Changamire Arms
by
Robin Walker

Lovecraft's Masters of Humorous Prose
by
Thaddeus Lovecraft

Rum Humour/Rum Humor
by
Thaddeus Lovecraft

Books available on Amazon.com
and
In all good bookshops

ABOUT THE AUTHORS

Nick Faulder was born in West London in the vicinity of Wormwood Scrubs prison. Using a combination of wile, guile and women's clothing, he managed to avoid a term of incarceration during his infant years – a rare feat for the 1950's when prison staff actively recruited potential young inmates with street campaigns, mime and bags of sweets. At seven years old he vanished, re-emerging in Ramsgate forty years later – Nick's dark ages, he calls them, although rumour has it that he changed colour for a while. On his return to normal life, Nick took up writing, mainly on walls and tube trains, progressing to become a personal assistant to William Posters.

Shortly after this, disaster struck when he was diagnosed with *Genetic Crottage*, which affected his ability to construct meaningful sentences. Life took another downward turn when he experienced writer's block. Fortuitously, it was when confined to the writer's block in Budleigh Salterton Sanatorium that Nick met Thaddeus Lovecraft, recovering from an overdose of writing incomprehensible tosh.

The two hit it off immediately. Nick says he doesn't mind Lovecraft threatening him to write at the point of a gun, quote: 'Thad's a great guy, a real megalomaniac – love him t' bits.'

It is believed that **Thaddeus Lovecraft** was born in Ireland sometime between January 1965 and October 1972. Although some researchers cling fast to the claim that he was home-schooled, there is growing support for the theory that he received no formal education whatsoever.

Notwithstanding this limitation, he entered Trinity College Dublin in September 1990. Later that day he was asked to leave as they were closing up for the night.

The rest of Lovecraft's life is shrouded in mystery. His parents were killed in a freak hairdressing accident, allowing him to use his vast inheritance to protect himself from the outside world forever.

Several mail-order brides were bought with his credit card in March 1997 but all were returned in their original packaging before the 28-day period had elapsed.